The
LAST LIGHT
of DELHI

The
LAST LIGHT
of DELHI

Glimpses from a Golden Age of Poetry

Mirza
Farhatullah Baig

Translated *from the Urdu by*
SULAIMAN AHMAD *and* PARVATI SHARMA

With an Introduction by SULAIMAN AHMAD

PENGUIN BOOKS
An imprint of Penguin Random House

PENGUIN BOOKS

USA | Canada | UK | Ireland | Australia
New Zealand | India | South Africa | China

Penguin Books is part of the Penguin Random House group of companies
whose addresses can be found at global.penguinrandomhouse.com

Published by Penguin Random House India Pvt. Ltd
4th Floor, Capital Tower 1, MG Road,
Gurugram 122 002, Haryana, India

First published in English in Penguin Books by Penguin Random House India 2022

Introduction copyright © Sulaiman Ahmad
English translation copyright © Sulaiman Ahmad and Parvati Sharma 2022

ISBN 9780670094257

Typeset in Bembo Std by Manipal Technologies Limited, Manipal
Printed at Replika Press Pvt. Ltd, India

www.penguin.co.in

In memory of my brother Doctor S. Husan Ahmad, who was waiting for this book so eagerly but alas, taken by the pandemic, could not see this book in print.

It is also my fond hope that this work will be read by my grandchildren, Saadia, Imran and Nylah, and that it will give them a glimpse of our cultural heritage.

Contents

Introduction

by Sulaiman Ahmad

Aah Dilli!

Marsiya Dilli ye marhoom ka ae dost na cher
Na sunaa jaaye-gaa hum se yeh fasaanaa hargiz

Do not, my friend, begin a dirge for Delhi deceased—
I will not be able to bear it, hearing this tale.

So laments Altaf Husain Hali, one of the greatest stalwarts of Urdu literature—a poet, critic, biographer, essayist and reformer. He was bemoaning the condition of Delhi after 1857.

His was not a new lament. Much like the Mughal empire, which had long made the city its capital, Delhi had been in a state of decline for decades, and mournful melodies about the gradual decay in the splendour and sophistication of the city had been composed by many bards. Mir Taqi Mir, who died a half-century before the final nail in the

coffin of the Mughal empire was struck in 1857, wrote in
his melancholic and wistful style:

Kooche jo thei Dilli ke auraaq e musawwir thei
Jo shakl nazar aye tasweer nazar ayee

The lanes of Delhi were sketches by artists,
the faces you looked at, the faces were portraits

It was Mir, too, who composed a famous response to jibes
during his visit to Lucknow, where fashionable Luckhnowis
made fun of his old-fashioned Delhi style, not knowing that
it was the venerable Mir they were mocking.

Kya bood-o-bash poocho ho purab ke sakino
Hum ko ghareeb jaan ke hans-hans pukar ke
    Dilli jo ek shahr tha alam mein intekhab
    Rahte thie muntakhab hi jahan rozgaar ke
Us ko falak ne loot ke barbaad kar diya
Hum rahne wale hain usi ujre dayaar ke

What do you ask of me,* people of the east,
taking me to be poor, hurling laughter at me?
    Delhi once was the world's chosen city,
        where only the chosen of their times would reside—
That the stars have looted and destroyed,
and I am one from that ruined land.

                            *

---

* What do you ask of my identity, that is.

It is said of Delhi, or Dilli, that the city has been destroyed many times, only to rise from its own ashes, each time with new vigour. Indeed the city has a long history, going far into myth and legend. Many have wondered when the city was first established and who its inhabitants were, and this search takes one back several millennia to Hastinapur, the city of the Kurus in the *Mahabharata*. Two sets of brothers, the Pandavas and the Kauravas, fought to lead the Kuru clan, and a new settlement came up under the Pandavas. This was the legendary Indraprastha, a city so grand that it became the envy of its times. How and why it suddenly vanished is hidden in the shadows of the ancient past. Only its legends remain now.

However, it is said that, after a long gap, a king named Dhilu (or Dihlu) ruled the ancient habitation and gave it his name; thus the city was called Dilli. After this, there is another long gap, obscured by time. History opens its pages with King Anang Pal of the Tomara dynasty, who founded a city called Lal Kot, possibly in the eighth century, which was conquered and renamed Qila Rai Pithora by Prithviraj Chauhan in the twelfth. Soon after, however, in 1192, Chauhan was defeated by Muhammad Ghori, who left the city in the care of his general, Qutb-ud-din Aibak, the man who laid the foundations of the Qutub Minar, a tower that has been emblematic of Delhi from the thirteenth century until today. The cities of Anang Pal Tomara, Prithviraj Chauhan and Qutb-ud-din Aibak were the earliest of the many great cities of Delhi's past. Thereafter came different people and new dynasties, building the forts, palaces and townships of Siri, Tughlaqabad, Kotla Firoze Shah, the

Purana Qila and Shahjahanabad—and, of course, the 'new' Delhi in which so many of the city's current denizens now live.

These changes in location and architecture were also part of a more profound civilizational transformation. Dilli was growing increasingly prosperous, as people of all kinds thronged the city: Hindus, Muslims, Turks, Afghans, some of Hindustani stock, some of Irani. A city of crowded inns and taverns, and glamorous markets; every professional a master of his craft. Foreign and local colours had mixed and merged into one, producing a unique and pleasing new shade.

*

Such intermingling resulted in a new culture and civilization. Gradually a new language emerged. This had to happen. After all, no civilization is born dumb. The culture of the new civilization that developed and flourished was named the Ganga–Jamni culture, the culture of intermingling rivers, a confluence that reached its peak under the Mughals.

The Mughal empire lasted, in one way or another, from 1526—when Babur defeated Ibrahim Lodi on the fields of Panipat—to 1857, when the East India Company crushed its last remnants and sent its last emperor, Bahadur Shah Zafar, into exile.

In the interim, and at their height, the Mughals had built a grand empire, a glorious civilization and a prosperous and affluent economy. Literature, scholarship, music, painting and architecture flourished under their patronage. Although the early Mughals ruled from Agra or Lahore, Shahjahan—the emperor who built the Taj Mahal—gave Delhi its most glamorous age, building the magnificent city of Shahjahanabad.

As Mughal power declined, however, Delhi grew weak, destroyed and plundered many times as it lost its magnificence and lustre. As Mir puts it:

Ab kharaabaa huaa Jahanabad
Warna har ek qadam pe yaan ghar thaa

Now Jahanabad has become a barren yard,
though once there was a home at every step.

The Dilli of Our Book

Jahanabad, or Shahjahanabad, is the name of that part of Delhi that was laid out by Shahjahan; today, it is the walled city often called 'old Delhi'. In 1837, when Bahadur Shah Zafar, the last Mughal, ascended his throne, Delhi was effectively ruled by the East India Company. Bahadur Shah was a ruler only in name, destined to watch the vestiges of his empire crumble as he lived out his last days in exile. But it is this Bahadur Shah who is, in a way, the hero of our story, alongside the Delhi that he 'ruled'. He sat on the Mughal emperor's throne, though not the grand peacock throne of Shahjahan, which had been looted by Nadir Shah decades ago. He was a puppet emperor, whose power did not extend beyond the Red Fort and the walled city, a king who lived on a pension fixed by the East India Company. And yet, though the empire barely existed any longer, its customs, traditions and conventions were still alive. Delhi was full of life and the best of every sphere would gather here to be a part of its rich social milieu. The Company made no objection to such hollow pomp and show; and so it was that, at the nadir of the empire, its culture was at its peak. All the refinement and delicacy of the five human senses were fully attended to and cultivated to the utmost. Delhi was still one of the biggest cultural and social centres of Asia.

A critical aspect of this cultural ambience was poetry. The style, polish and refinement of Delhi's language was now at its best. The greatest poets on the firmament of Urdu poetry happened to live and flourish during this period. The emperor himself was a fine poet.

On the other hand, while Delhi's poetic and cultural achievements reached new heights, its political fortunes were approaching a tragic low. The new rulers of the city, who would soon grab the reins of the empire, were quite different from the many others who had conquered and ruled Delhi. The city was used to destruction and new beginnings. So far, however, all those who conquered had also settled here, made this land their home and, thus, enriched it in many ways, even after destroying earlier kingdoms. This time it was different. The age of colonial imperialism, particularly as it developed after 1857, had come. A foreign power that would insist on remaining so, would rule from overseas, despoiling this land and enriching its own coffers, transferring the wealth of Hindustan to their island. Almost a corollary to the Company's greed was its contempt for local learning, education and culture. Delhi's obliteration was on the horizon.

This is the world that Mirza Farhatullah Baig's book tries to capture.

Although *Dilli ki Aakhri Shama* is overtly the narrative of a fictional mushaira, a symposium of poets, *circa* 1845, it has actually turned out to be much more than that. In fact, it is a cultural document of the period; a portrait of a civilization, of the life and living styles of the upper classes of Delhi in the decade before the fateful year 1857. Poetry was very much a part of this cultural milieu. As such, Baig's mushaira is a potrait of a culture and tradition.

The details of various aspects of cultural etiquette are described by Baig, even seemingly minor matters like seating arrangements at a mushaira, how the verses of another poet were appreciated, etc. Baig takes us into the sitting rooms of some of the great personalities of Delhi, from Mirza Ghalib to Bahadur Shah Zafar, allowing us a glimpse of their private lives. Only a person who had made a deep study of the life and cultural atmosphere of Delhi and the Red Fort at the time could have portrayed the vivid details of language and manners, dress and decoration as Baig does.

As for the poets themselves, Baig has described their homes, their manners, their dress and ways of talking with such skill, filling his portraits with colour and detail so that the poets appear vividly before us. And he does not stop there, but also describes their style of reciting in the mushaira, so that it seems as if each poet is speaking out from the pages of the book.

Mirza Farhatullah Baig (1883–1947)

The creator of this vivid and vibrant vignette of Mughal Delhi, Mirza Farhatullah Baig, was himself quite a colourful person too.

He lived and wrote at the turn of the nineteenth century, a time that may be called a period of transition in Indian history. People of his days looked back to the pre-1857 cultural milieu with a sense of nostalgia, and viewed its passing with regret and a feeling of loss. In Baig's writing, these bygone times are reimagined in all their glory. At the same time, conscious of the decline and ultimate defeat of this cultural sophistication, Mirza Baig, like many of his times, seemed to be living somewhere between the struggle of two worlds: the past pitted against the alien culture of new rulers. The old colour was fading, but the new was yet to take over.

Born in Delhi in 1883, twenty-six years after the uprising of 1857, Baig's early education was in a madarsa attached to a mosque near the dargah of Hazrat Nizamuddin Aulia. There he took elementary lessons from Syed Waliullah Dehlvi, known as Baghdadi, a famous local aalim, scholar, who spent his time educating children. At the age of nine, Baig went to a primary school and then to a high school in the neighbourhood of Kashmiri Gate. He earned a good name in the school, partly thanks to his abilities as a sportsman, partly because of his sense of humour, jovial temperament and participation in general school activities. He passed out of school with distinction.*

Thereafter, he was admitted to Hindu College, which had been established recently in Kinari Bazar, Chandni Chowk. The fee was a moderate two rupees per month, which suited Baig's difficult financial situation. However, it transpired that the college's own finances were almost as precarious as Baig's, which resulted in the exit of many good teachers, especially from the Faculty of Science and Mathematics. It was a frustrating situation for Baig, who wanted to become an engineer and was good at mathematics. Even so, he completed his intermediate degree from Hindu College; then left for a bachelor's degree at St Stephen's.

In St Stephen's, where Baig began to study in 1903, he changed his subject from science to Arabic. Why and how is another story, of which Baig has given a most delightful account in his classic *Maulvi Nazeer Ahmad ki Kahaani*—a book about the life and times of a Delhi stalwart, and of the Delhi of those days. In brief, the story Baig tells goes thus: his scientific ambitions having suffered yet another blow, Baig was convinced by a friend to enrol in Arabic classes, delivered by a pious professor, more involved in spiritual pursuits than in his classes, who left them soon after the

---

* Much of this biographical information on Baig is sourced from introductions to two editions of *Dilli ki Aakhri Shama*: one by Dr Salahuddin (Urdu Academy, Delhi, 1986) and the other by Rasheed Hasan Khan (Anjuman Taraqqi-e Urdu, 2009), which also includes a foreword by Khaliq Anjum.

two friends had joined his class. Baig and his friend were then told to find their own teacher, and thus came to lurk on the steps of Delhi's Jama Masjid in the hope of trapping an unsuspecting maulvi. In the end, it was Maulvi Nazeer Ahmad—an early luminary of modern Urdu prose—whom they found and persuaded to teach them. Much later, Baig wrote a slim sketch of the man who became his mentor, and launched his own literary career in the process.

At St Stephen's, Baig was popular with both his classmates and his professors. A bright student, good athlete and swimmer, active dramatist and debater, excellent cricketer and tennis player, he caught the particular attention of Professor C. F. Andrews (who was both an active ally of the growing freedom struggle in India and had played cricket for Cambridge). Baig passed his BA examination with distinction and took admission for an MA at the same college. However, despite help from Professor Andrews, he could not complete his master's because of financial constraints.

Baig left Delhi in 1908 to join a government school in Hyderabad. About a year or so thereafter, he got an opportunity to enter a type of paralegal service when he was appointed a translator in the Hyderabad High Court. During this time, he took and passed the judicial examination and rose through the ranks until, eventually, he reached the level of an inspecting officer at the high court, a rank equivalent to that of a high court judge today.

Baig was a multifaceted personality. Even amidst his heavy duties and busy official life, he cultivated many hobbies. A prolific writer, he was also fond of painting, photography, dramatics and poetry, and tried his hand at each of these arts.

He was a handsome man, tall, well-exercised and broad-shouldered, with a longish, oval face, broad forehead, bright eyes and aquiline nose. He sported a moustache, but would shave his beard every day.

On this particular habit, he wrote, with his usual sense of humour:

Daadhi to mundaate ho mochen bhi mundaa daalo
Tab nikle gi aye Farhat kuch surat-e mardaanaa

You shave your beard already, shave your moustache as well,
only then will emerge, O Farhat, something of a man's face.

He disliked Western clothes. When compelled to wear any, he would take them off as soon as possible and return to his sherwani. Pump shoes (what would be called 'loafers' today, shoes without laces), worn without socks, were his regular footwear.

Though Baig would never live in Delhi after his college days, he remembered the city with nostalgia. And yet, whenever he did manage to visit Delhi, he would be unable to reconcile himself with the changes that were taking over his old city. He writes of Delhi's past as though pining for it. Many of his books—*Dilli ki Aakhri Shama, Phool Waalon ki Sair, Maulvi Nazeer Ahmad ki Kahaani*, and his account of his own early days in Delhi—include wonderfully vivid sketches and colourful portraits of those times, as if in memoriam to his beloved city.

His personality itself was a memory of Delhi.

What Triggered the Idea of this Book?

The immediate trigger was a portrait of Hakeem Momin Khan that Mirza Farhatullah Baig came across. 'The moment I saw the portrait, the idea came to me,' writes Baig, 'you too . . . create a mushaira.'[*]

He felt that soon a time would come when no one would remember the extraordinary personalities who had been the brightest stars in the Delhi sky just decades ago. 'A day will come,' he wrote, 'when no one will be able to tell you where Momin lived, just as no one except I, perhaps, know where he is buried.' It struck him that he might create sketches of those times, as if on a canvas, in which people like Momin and his contemporaries would appear going about their daily lives. These snapshots would appear as running pictures of the lives and times of those persons—as if being watched in a movie.

A cousin of Baig's, Mirza Asmatullah Baig, has written of how Baig had a taste for dastan-goi, storytelling.[†] He

---

[*] From Baig's own preface to *Dilli ki Aakhri Shama*.

[†] Referenced by Dr Salahuddin in his introduction to an edition of *Dilli ki Aakhri Shama* published by the Urdu Academy, Delhi, 1986.

had grown up hearing tales of magic and wizardry from the old ladies of his house, and would later retell these stories, adding new layers and scenes, delighting his audiences with his vivid and lively narrations.

His cousin felt that perhaps this background of Baig's helped him visualize the kind of drama that might unfold from a simple collection of character sketches, and which resulted in this masterpiece of literature.

Now, with Momin's portrait as his immediate inspiration and his flair for storytelling, Baig was also influenced by two books. One was Mohammad Hussain Azad's *Nairang-iye Khayal* ('A Wonder-world of Thoughts'). Azad, a writer of poetry and prose in the nineteenth century, had featured an imaginary mushaira in this book, set in the court of Bahadur Shah Zafar, along with digressions into the lives of various historical figures, from Chenghiz Khan to Kalidas.

The second literary influence on Baig was a famous *tazkiraa* ('narrative') by Maulvi Karimuddin, called *Tabqaat-e Shoara-e Hind* ('Biographies of the Poets of Hindustan') which was published in 1847 and included extensive descriptions of many poets. Most importantly, Karimuddin's *tazkiraa* also included a detailed description of a mushaira that took place in Rajab 1261 AH—that is, July or August 1845.

In order to write accurately about contemporary poets and literary figures, Maulvi Karimuddin would hold mushairas in his house twice a month and record accounts of them, including the ghazals recited and his thoughts on their authors. Thus, he had compiled a commendable literary history of the period.

Combining Azad's and Maulvi Saheb's works, Baig laid the foundations of his own fictitious mushaira. He has admitted his sources freely, and also that he gathered further anecdotes from Azad's *Aab-e Hayaat* ('Elixir of Life', a seminal history of Urdu poetry), and from conversations with people who lived in those times and the oral traditions that had been handed down to him.

However, while making use of these sources, Baig does not allow himself to be shackled by them in any way. Thus, while he often quotes the same ghazals that were recited in Maulvi Karimuddin's work, and provides similar descriptions of some poets, he offers a straightforward and dramatic narration, quite unlike Maulvi Karimuddin's rather dense, academic treatise. Time is not a constraint for him either. For instance, Dagh Dehlvi, a future great poet of this tradition, would have been nowhere on the scene on the date of Baig's mushaira, but Baig introduces him into it nevertheless.

Baig acknowledges his debt to Maulvi Karimuddin—naming his own narrator after the maulvi, and setting his mushaira on the very date, 20 July 1845, when Maulvi Saheb hosted a mushaira at his own home. Of course, this historical mushaira was on a very small scale, and Baig writes, in the foreword to his book, that he changed the original mushaira's scale, canvas and ambience totally, presenting it as a key literary event in Delhi. Baig also mentions that the fact of Zain-ul-Abdeen Khan Arif (Ghalib's nephew, and poet in his own right) attending Karimuddin's mushaira gave Baig the idea of making Arif his catalyst, the key to arranging the mushaira of his book.

With characteristic humour, Baig writes that he could have put himself as the narrator of his book, but he did not feel like ignoring all the hard work done by Maulvi Saheb. Using an Urdu proverb, he says it would be like removing a fly that has fallen into a cup of milk.* He adds, tongue in cheek, that if there are shortcomings in his work, the blame should be passed on to Maulvi Saheb. 'Here, now, I appear in the garb of Maulvi Karimuddin, but I do say this,' he writes, 'that since I'm offering all my hard work to Maulvi Karimuddin, whatever good or bad you may have to say about this book, don't say it to me—say it to Maulvi Saheb, and say it to your heart's content. I will be happy, and my God too!'

A Note on the Ghazal

At any mention of Urdu poetry, the ghazal is the first thing that comes to mind. It is especially so for mushairas, as the life and vitality of a mushaira comes from ghazals. An overwhelming number of the poems in this book are ghazals. It may be apt, therefore, to talk a little about the ghazal, the most popular form of Urdu poetry, almost its soul.

The ghazal is indeed a strange species. The actual meaning of the word is *sukhan ba mashooq*, that is, talking to the beloved. Some renowned ghazal poets have

---

* An idiom with exactly the opposite sense of 'fly in the ointment'. In this case, the sympathy is with the fly; that is, Karimuddin's work was substantial, and to remove him from the milk would be to grab all the milk unfairly.

demonstrated this in their couplets in most exquisite ways.
Momin Khan Momin, a master of the ghazal and Ghalib's
contemporary, says:

> *Tum mere paas hote ho goya*
> *Jab koi doosraa naheen hotaa*

> It is as if you are close to me
> when there is no one else.

He addresses his *mashooq*, beloved, with a touch of sarcasm:

> *Hum samajhte hain aazmane ko*
> *Uzr kuch chaahiye sataane ko*

> I know you do it as if you're testing me,
> for you need an excuse to torment me.

Another:

> *Shab tum jo bazm e ghair mein aankhen chora gaye*
> *Khoye gaye hum aise, ke aghyaar paa gaye*

> Last night when you would not look at me in *ghair's**
> gathering,
> so lost was I, others found out my love.

---

* The *ghair* is the poet's rival for the heart of the beloved, the *mashooq*. More
on such recurring tropes later.

This aspect of the ghazal addressing the beloved has remained alive through the ages. Thus, the modern poet Firaq Gorakhpuri:

Tum mokhaatib bhi ho qareeb bhi ho
Tum ko dekhein ke tum se baat karein

You speak and you are close by too,
should I stare at you or talk to you?

And Faiz Ahmad Faiz:

Tum ko dekha to chashm ser hue
Tum ko chaahaa to aur chaah na ki

I saw you and my eyes were satiated,
I loved no further after I loved you.

The definition of mashooq, the beloved, has been extended to endless limits, however, as we shall see.

For all its popularity, the ghazal has faced its share of severe criticism. At worst, it has been flayed as a 'semi-savage form of poesy', criticized for its limited scope and canvas, its overemphasis on the same old, worn-out subjects and metaphors through a restricted medium.[*] The description of beloveds was found to be so similar and hackneyed that

---

[*] The twentieth-century scholar and critic Kaleemuddin Ahmad described the ghazal as a 'neem-wahshi sinf-e-sukhan', a semi-savage form of poesy.

it was said that if both father and son happened to be poets, which was often the case, the similes they employed would make it seem as if both were in love with the same mashooq. Even Ghalib, perhaps the most famous poet of the language and a poet, primarily, of ghazals, complained:

Naheen ba harf-e bayaan zarf-e tangnaa-e ghazal
Kuch aur chaahiye wusat mere beyaan ke liye

The ghazal's narrow form won't suffice for my speech,
I need a greater canvas to give my full account.

For all the criticisms and even movements against it by some modern writers, however, the ghazal has continued to rule unabated and no mushaira can be considered complete without it.

Indeed, the ghazal has also proved, in the course of time, that it is capable of changing its vocabulary, expressions and diction with changing circumstances, social conditions and sensibilities. Some modern poets have used the ghazal very effectively to address changing situations in different and difficult times. The Partition of the subcontinent, for instance, left a deep sense of trauma among the people affected by it. Some of these verses could be called representative of new expressions used to address this pain.

The following couplet by an unknown modern Pakistani poet, with its peculiar pathos about this personal sense of tragedy, has captured the pain of a generation:

Manzil to khair kya thi hamaare naseeb mein
Itna hua ke ghar se bahut door aa gaye

My fate held no destination in any case!
Only this happened: that I came so far from home.

Professor Wajeehuddin, who composes poetry under the name of Shehper Rasool, writes:

Mujhe bhi lamha-e hijrat ne kar diya taqseem
Nigaah ghar ki taraf hai, qadam safar ki taraf

I too was divided by the moment of migration:
my eyes face home, my feet face the journey.

Yet another modern poet, Juan Ellia, laments:

Go main bagola bun ke bikhra waqt ki pagal andhi mein,
Kya main tumhari lahr naheen hoon Ganga ji aur Jumana ji

Though I was scatterd like a whirlwind in the mad tempest of times,
am I not a wave of yours, Ganga ji and Jamuna ji?

Another change to the ghazal came with the participation of women in the genre. Earlier, even if women entered the field of poetry, they had to remain 'hidden' behind a pseudonym, and stick to the masculine gender in their compositions, like male poets. With the movement of feminism, or 'nuswaniyat' in Urdu, women poets began to express themselves clearly and strongly, as women, using the feminine gender, and conveying their sense of rebellion, anger, supressed emotions or urge for liberation.

Thus, Parveen Shakir writes:

Main sach kahoongi magar phir bhi haar jaaoongi
Woh jhoot bolega or lajawaab kar dega

Even if I speak the truth, I will lose;
He will lie with such confidence that all arguments will fail.

Bas yun hua ke us ne takalluf se baat ki
Aur main ne rote-rote dupatte bhigo liye

It only happened that he spoke a little formally,
and I wept and I wept till my *dupattas* were soaked.

A fine example of feminine sensibility, representative of women's socio-cultural situation.

*

Now, let us see how a ghazal is composed. The ghazal's 'building blocks' are couplets, called 'shers'. All the couplets must follow the same metre, and a rhyming scheme whereby the penultimate words of every couplet rhyme (this rhyme is called the 'qafia'), while the last word of every couplet is repeated (this is the 'radeef').

The other main components of a ghazal are the 'matla' and the 'maqta'. A ghazal's first couplet is called the 'matla'. The matla will use rhyming qafias in both its lines, along with the radeef. If the second couplet follows this scheme, it is called a 'husn-e matla'.

Some ghazals do not have a repeated radeef and they are called 'ghair muraddaf'. This is rare, however, since it is the radeef that brings beauty, music and depth to a ghazal and, therefore, few ghazals in Urdu are without one. The rhyme of the qafia is essential to a ghazal, and no ghazal does without it.

A ghazal's concluding couplet is called the 'maqta', and it usually features the poet's name. Naming oneself in the maqta is customary though not essential.

A ghazal requires no fixed number of couplets, but generally there are five, seven or nine. The odd number is traditionally used to indicate the uniqueness of the beloved (that is, with no match) as also the agony of the eternal separation of the lover from the beloved.

The uniqueness of the ghazal, what distinguishes it from other forms of poetry, is that every couplet is independent and complete in itself. It has no connection with previous or later couplets; indeed, the theme of the next couplet could be totally different, with no bearing on what has preceded it. This aspect of the ghazal, which gives it the appearance of a bunch of scattered thoughts brought together by rhyme, has also met with severe criticism.

However, what is overlooked by these criticisms is the inner nature and the unrevealed mechanisms of the ghazal. The ghazal is the perfection of the art of using allusions to make meaning. Thus, to create a precise yet highly interpretable meaning in two lines becomes an art in itself. In a ghazal, the poet's expressions are not confined to the literal sense of the words employed, but venture far from the confines of strict meaning, via metaphors, similes and allusions, creating new worlds of meaning. In the hands of a master ghazal poet, each sher contains multitudes of allusions and implications; the poet's skill, as the Urdu saying goes, lies in 'pouring a river into a pot'.

Sometimes, however, there can be ghazals of a different type. If a thought cannot be expressed in one couplet, it is expanded in two or even three. In that case, that portion of the ghazal is called a 'qata'. Poets have also used ghazals to express one unified thought through all its verses. Such ghazals are called 'ghazl-e musalsal', that is, a continuous ghazal. Its face is that of a ghazal, but it is more akin to a straightforward poem, or 'nazm'.

The great masters have used the medium of the ghazal in exquisite ways to articulate complex human thoughts, philosophical concepts, revolutionary ideals, and, of course, the universal emotions of humankind—all in two precise lines.

The ultimate master, Mir, who has often been called 'khuda-e sukhan', the god of poesy, ponders:

Aalam kasoo hakeem ka bandha tilism hai
Kuch ho to etbaar bhi ho kainaat ka

The universe is the illusion of some wisecrack,
One could have faith if something was there in fact.

A complex thought about a metaphysical situation on which volumes of philosophy have been written, stated in simple language. The Matrix series of movies come to mind!

Masters have expressed such surprising, wonderful and vast range of thoughts without stepping out of the universe of the ghazal or forsaking its diction. Given their structure, couplets have a naturally aphoristic quality; and often enough, a poet's concise articulation of a thought or emotion experienced by him transcends the couplet to attain the status of a proverb. This has been called 'sehl mumtani'.

Ghazals have included endless plays on the concepts of 'mashooq', the beloved, and 'ishq', love. At the metaphysical level, mashooq often becomes the primordial reality, the divine; and ishq a passion for God and all His manifestations. Over different ages, the concepts of mashooq and ishq have also offered commentaries on an ideal of humanity, a cherished society, just or tyrannical socio-political orders. Other recurring tropes of the ghazal—the lover's rival and the tavern-keeper, the jar of wine and the brimming cup, figures from legends and literature—have also appeared in different garbs. As Ghalib says:

Harchand ho mushaada-e haq ki guftogoo
Banti naheen hai saaghar-o meena kahe beghair

Though the talk may well be of witnessing truth,
without talk of goblets and jars, it will not flow.

And:

> *Maqsad ho naz-o-naam, wale guftogoo mein kaam*
> *Chalta nahin hai khanjar-o-dishna kahe baghair*

The subject may be of grace and coquetry,
it won't work without saying 'knife and dagger'.

And Faiz, a century later:

> *Jaan jaayenge jaanne waale*
> *Faiz Farhad-o Jum ke baat karein*

Those who know will understand;
Faiz, let us talk of Farhad and Jam.*

This adept handling of the medium by the masters, however, has created a little problem too. Often, minor poets manage to imitate the masters, and sometimes do so tolerably well, so as to create the illusion of good poetry. When repeated by many, however, subjects are worn out and expressions become hackneyed and clichéd. The poets may be happy with their work but, for discerning critics, it would be difficult to determine their worth. In a nazm, on the other hand, it is easier to determine a poet's ability since it is easier to ascertain what is being said. All of this, however, does

---

* Farhad, a legendary hero and lover, and Jam (Jamshed), a mythological Persian king, are recurring characters in ghazals.

not mean that new thoughts are not being introduced in ghazals. In some modern ghazals, topical themes do crop up and a new vocabulary is being used to deal with them.

Because of its very nature, of conveying an idea in two lines, the ghazal remains hugely popular in modern mushairas also. An audience can react to each couplet as it is uttered, so that an immediate rapport is established and maintained throughout the ghazal. Appreciation (or booing, as the case may be) follows each couplet, and the mushaira remains nothing if not lively. Yet, it would perhaps be true to say that no modern poet has yet composed ghazals of the kind that once addressed topical themes with the kind of diction and emotion that bring a lasting universality.

Four Major Poets from Baig's Mushaira

Of all the poets who feature in Baig's mushaira, perhaps four deserve special mention.

Zauq: Sheikh Mohammad Ibrahim 'Zauq' (1790–1854)

Zauq is a good example of how a poet's status and worth oscillates with changing times, and the temperaments, intellectual bearings and sensibilities of new ages.

In his own time, Zauq was the ustad—teacher, master— of his emperor and, in fact, of the entire Qila—the Red Fort—over which Emperor Bahadur Shah Zafar ruled. His position may be compared to that of a poet laureate. In short, Zauq was considered the pre-eminent poet of his times.

It is said that his ancestors came from a Hindu Khatri family. Zauq's father, Sheikh Muhammad Ramzan, was a poor sepoy. Muhammad Husain Azad* writes that the Sheikh was an ordinary man who had studied from the book of life and could talk about many matters with much understanding. He lived near Kabuli Darwaza (now the Khooni Darwaza, in Delhi) and was employed in the haram-sara, the women's quarters, of one Nawab Lutf Ali Khan, who evidently thought of the Sheikh as a capable and reliable person. Only the most loyal, diligent and trustworthy persons would be employed in a position of such familiarity.

For his early education, Zauq—or Mohammad Ibrahim, which was his name—was sent to the local madarsa run by Hafiz Ghulam Rasool. As was the fashion in those days, Hafiz Saheb was fond of poetry and happened to indulge in it himself, using the pen name 'Shauq', meaning 'interest' or 'inclination'. It is said that it was 'Shauq' who inspired Ibrahim to adopt the name 'Zauq'— 'taste, discernment'— for himself.

Gradually, along with other students who were influenced by Ghulam Rasool's poetic activities, Zauq developed a passion for this art. With his sharp memory, he

---

* Muhammad Husain Azad, a writer of poetry and prose, is best known for his *Aab-e Hayaat* ('The Water of Life'), a history of Urdu poetry and poets. Much of the biographical information on Zauq, here, has been sourced from Azad's seminal work.

was able to remember hundreds of verses, though his own compositions did not flow so easily. Azad writes that Zauq told him that he finally managed to compose his first two verses at the age of thirteen or fourteen. The first of these was a 'hamd', praise of Allah; and the second a 'naat', praise of the Prophet. At the time he was hardly able to appreciate the significance of his choice of poetic styles, but this should have been taken as a good omen.

After some time, like many others, he showed his work to Shah Naseer, the pre-eminent ustad of his times. However, for reasons unknown, there was little collaboration or engagement between the ustad and the budding poet, and the arrangement did not last long.

Nor does Zauq seem to have received unmitigated encouragement from his teacher, Hafiz Ghulam Rasool. Once, he composed a ghazal that borrowed the qafia and radeef from a famous ghazal by the great eighteenth-century poet, Sauda. When he showed his work to Hafiz Saheb, the teacher was very cross and threw the paper away, admonishing him for trying to imitate a master. However, at the insistence of some other elders who had seen this ghazal, Zauq went ahead and recited it at a mushaira, where it was highly acclaimed.

Increasingly, Zauq began going to mushairas independently, without having his ghazals vetted by any ustad.

The acceptance, reception and appreciation he received were great. His ghazals soon became so popular that they drew the attention of songsters too, and were sung in Delhi's houses and lanes. With his mastery over the language and his choice of poetic themes that suited the temperament of that age, he was soon considered an ustad himself.

At the age of eighteen or so he composed the following matla:

Maathe pe tere chamke hai jhoomar ka para chaand
Laa bosa charhe chaand ka wada tha chadhaa chand

On your forehead glimmers the *jhoomar** of the moon,
a kiss now: it was promised with the moon, and here's
the moon!

'Chaand chadnaa' was an idiomatic turn of phrase for a full moon, considered informal and peculiar to the vocabulary of women at the time. To use what might be called 'slang' in formal verse intended for a courtly audience would have required considerable skill and confidence from Zauq, and demonstrated great flair, especially given that he was a young and unknown poet at the time.

Zauq was now an established ustad, but he wasn't satisfied. Seeking wider recognition, he began to look for ways to introduce himself into the court within the Red Fort. Finally, through some contacts, he was able to reach the circle of Prince Abu Zafar, a keen poet.

---

* A 'jhoomar' is a chandelier and also the name of a piece of jewellery worn by women on the forehead. Hence the simile of 'chaand chadhnaa'—the moon rising on your brow.

Mohammad Husain Azad writes that, one day, when Zauq came to him, the prince was practising archery. When he saw Zauq, he complained that Ustad Shah Naseer had left for the Deccan and that even Zauq was not visiting him often enough. The unhappy prince took out a newly composed ghazal from his pocket and handed it to Zauq. Zauq sat down and made his changes and corrections then and there.

This was much appreciated, and gradually Zauq became very close to Prince Abu Zafar, who appointed him his ustad, with a monthly salary of four rupees.

Zauq's father was not in favour of this service. Moreover, Abu Zafar's own position in court was precarious at that time. Akbar Shah, the then emperor, was said to favour another son as his heir; and the matter of succession was pending before the East India Company. As a result, Abu Zafar was not getting his full pension. In this uncertain situation, Zauq's father advised him against taking a position with a disfavoured prince, that too for such a small a salary. However, Zauq trusted his fate—and the fate of Abu Zafar.

His gamble paid off. It was indeed Abu Zafar who became the future Bahadur Shah, the next and last Mughal Emperor.

Now, as the Badshah's ustad, Zauq's position and status as a poet was unparalleled. His loyalty, too, did not go unappreciated: Bahadur Shah would give his favourite poet grand titles such as 'Khaqani-e Hind' ('the Khaqani of Hindustan'—Khaqani was a famous, twelfth-century Persian poet, considered a master of the qasida, ode, for which Zauq, too, had a special talent) and 'Malik-ush Shoara' ('King of Poets').

Zauq's linguistic craft was distinguished. With his simple yet beautifully knit diction, and his imaginative use of idioms, he enjoyed a unique position in his age. He could use long and complicated qafias in his ghazals with considerable ease:

> *Bulbul hoon sehne baagh se door aur shikastaa per*
> *Parvana hoon chiraagh se door aur shikastaa per*

> I am a nightingale, from the garden afar, and with broken wings;
> I am a moth, from the lamp afar, and with broken wings.

Here, 'se door aur shikasataa per'—'afar, and with broken wings' is the qafia—to use it in every single one of the ghazal's couplets is a considerable feat.

Some of Zauq's best couplets, with their lucid language and deep emotion, would move anyone:

> *Layee hayaat aaye, qazaa le chali chale*
> *Apni khushi na aaye, na apni khushi chale*

> Life brings me along, I come; death takes me away, I go;
> I did not come of my own account, nor do I so go.

> *Ab to ghabraa key yeh kahte hain ke mar jaayenge*
> *Mar ke bhi chain na paaya to kidhar jaayenge*

.Now in despair, I say I shall die,
　　but if in death I despair, where shall I lie?

It is a legend that, on hearing this couplet, Ghalib exclaimed that he would gladly exchange all his works for this one bit of verse.

Zauq was adept at every form of poetry that was prevalent in his time but, if there is a form that may be considered his forte, it is the qasida, a kind of ode. In this form, only Sauda— the eighteenth-century poet whom Zauq had once imitated to his teacher's dismay—may be considered his equal.

Besides poetry, Zauq's interests were music and astrology. He had a deep knowledge of these subjects, as well as of Islamic mysticism and jurisprudence, Quranic tafseer (commentaries) and history. He was fluent in Arabic and Persian, as well as Urdu.

However, his main interest and skill was in poetry; and he was fortunate in that he could also make poetry his vocation. Bahadur Shah's patronage ensured that he— unlike many of his contemporaries—lived free of financial difficulties and could spend all his time in perfecting the art to which he was devoted.

Mohammad Husain Azad, who was a devoted shagrid, disciple, of Zauq's, has given an interesting account of how his ustad's works survived him. According to Azad, Zauq never cared much to arrange his verses. (He makes another outlandish comment that Zauq wrote the ghazals that Bahadur Shah recited as his own—a claim that has been rejected by all noted critics and researchers.)

Be that as it may, Azad writes that Zauq had crammed all his ghazals in a bag, or some such folder, in which they lay haphazard. The bag came to Azad when the great poet died in 1854, aged sixty-five.

Three years later, in the turmoil of 1857, the city was under siege and everyone was trying to escape with his life, Azad amongst them. No one could escape with more than they could carry and Azad was in a turmoil, wondering what he should take with him. His eyes fell on the papers of Zauq, and he thought that everything else could be acquired again, but his ustad would never come back. So, he picked up that bag, fleeing with it held to his chest. Eventually, he would arrange these poems into the diwan—the collected works—of his ustad, though many of Zauq's fine ghazals had been lost during Azad's escape, he claimed. A moving account, no doubt.

*Ghalib: Mirza Asadullah Khan 'Ghalib' (1797–1869)**

A line from one of Ghalib's Persian ghazals has proved to be prophetic:

---

* Frances W. Pritchett's 'A Desertful of Roses' is a wonderful online resource on Ghalib's life and poetry. Much of the biographical information on Ghalib, here, was sourced from this site, as also from two other works: *Tafhim-o-Tabir* by Khalid Mahmood and *Ghalib: Ma'ni-Afrini, Jadliyaati Waza', Shunyata aur Sheriyaat* ('Ghalib: Meaning, Mind, Dialectical Thought & Poetics') by Gopi Chand Narang.

Shohrat-e sheram ba geeti baad man khahad shudan

The fame of my poetry will spread to the world only once I am gone.

Though Ghalib was appreciated well enough during his lifetime, it is also a fact that the kind of admiration, even veneration, that burst upon him after his demise, did not exist while he lived—and he craved it.

In fact, not only did he not receive the acclaim that is now habitually showered upon him, in certain quarters he was even mocked for his unusual and unconventional writing style and diction. He was also denigrated for his thoughts and condemned for his free-spirited and unorthodox life. And, much to Ghalib's chagrin and dismay, it was Zauq who, as the emperor's ustad, enjoyed the status of poet laureate. Most likely, Ghalib, who was conscious of his worth, found this difficult to accept.

Today, he is not only universally admired by readers of Urdu poetry, but he also holds a place of pride in world literature. Most famously, the renowned modern poet, Muhammad Iqbal, compared him to the German writer and Ghalib's contemporary, Johann Wolfgang von Goethe, writing:

Aah tu ujdi hui Dilli mein araameeda hai
Gulshan-e Veemar mein teraa hamnavaa khwabidaa hai

Aah, as you repose in the ruins of Delhi,
so in Weimar's gardens your brother sleeps.

Faiz Ahmed Faiz, himself among the great poets of the twentieth century, said that 'Nobody can claim that they have read enough of Ghalib.' Faiz professed to keep a copy of Ghalib's works by his bedside at all times and use him in his own poetry both consciously and unconsciously.

All this came after Ghalib's demise, however. In his own time, he lamented that he was not appreciated enough. Like the prophetic Persian line on page xli, another couplet of Ghalib's articulates this tragic disappointment of his life, that he was not sufficiently recognized:

Hoon garmi-e nishaat-e tasawur se naghmaa sanj
Main andleeb-e gulshan-e naafridaa hoon

I sing with the fevered happiness of my imagination,
I am the nightingale of a garden that is yet to be born.

This, however, does not mean that there were not enough votaries for Ghalib in his life.

Born in the year 1796 in Agra, Ghalib's full name was Asadullah Beg Khan. Mirza Nausha was his alias or nickname, and he was bestowed the titles Najmuddaula, Dabeerul Mulk and Nizam-e-Jang ('Star of the State', 'Secretary of the State' and 'Strategic Organizer') by the Mughal court. These honorifics meant a symbolic incorporation of Ghalib into the ranks of Delhi's nobility. It was Bahadur Shah, too, who titled him Mirza Nausha ('mirza' being 'prince' or 'young nobleman', and 'nausha', 'fortunate'). He was appointed ustad, tutor, to the emperor in 1854, after Zauq's demise.

Ghalib's father, Mirza Ubaidullah Baig, died when Ghalib was a child, and he was brought up by his uncle, Mirza Nasrullah Baig. He received his early education in Agra. At the age of thirteen, he was married to Umrao Begum, daughter of Nawab Elahi Baksh Khan; and later he settled in Delhi, which was the most popular seat of poetry and poets.

This suited Ghalib very much. He had been fond of poetry from his childhood, and Delhi was the perfect city in which to incubate his talents. Initially, he had adopted the pen name 'Asad', but changed it to Ghalib later. An interesting anecdote has been cited for this change.

It is said that someone recited a couplet by an insignificant but rather flashy poet who had also adopted the pen name Asad (literally, 'lion'). The innocent reciter was under the impression that the couplet was by Ghalib himself:

Asad is jafaa per buton se wafa ki
Mere sher shabash rahmat khuda ki

Asad, despite the torment, you were loyal to the *but**
my lion, bravo, may you be blessed by God.

Ghalib was disgusted at hearing this ordinary verse being attributed to him. He was always aiming for a distinctive voice, in which metaphors, similes and imagery were used to

---

* 'But' is 'idol', literally, and a metaphor for the beloved in Urdu ghazals. See the note on recurring tropes in the ghazal that follows.

create a range of complicated—not always comprehensible—meaning. Such commonplace and obvious imagery used to express such an ordinary idea was the very antithesis of Ghalib's style and temperament. On hearing the couplet, Ghalib is said to have exclaimed, 'If this verse is by some other Asad, indeed God's blessings and mercy on him, but, if I happen to be this Asad, God's curse on me.'

It was after this that he gave up his original pen name.

Ghalib claimed descent from the legendary king of Turan, Afrasiyab. He traced his more recent ancestry to his grandfather, Mirza Qoqan Beg, a Seljuk Turk who came to India from Samarqand in the mid-eighteenth century, joined the Mughal court and eventually settled in Agra. Ghalib's ancestors were martial people and achieved a reasonably good position in their new home, with a fairly substantial estate.

Ghalib alludes to this martial background in one of his couplets:

Sau pusht se hai peshai abaa sipahgari
Kuch shaeri zaria-e izzat naheen mujhe

A hundred generations of mine were soldiers,
professional poetry holds no honour for me.

Ghalib's maternal grandparents, too, were aristocrats, and his early childhood, therefore, was spent in opulence. It goes to his credit that, despite the plentiful luxury and the lack of strict guardians, or the immediate need to learn any skills, he desired and acquired a good education.

However, as times and circumstances changed, Ghalib lost his estates and their income; and, though he tried various means to retrieve them, he was compelled, eventually, to subsist on what he could earn from his poetic skills. Ghalib's famously spendthrift nature did not help matters. A well-known anecdote about the poet tells of how, approached by a young grandson for a little pocket money, he said something to this effect: 'Do you really expect to find meat in a kite's nest?'

Whatever Ghalib earned, that is, was soon spent.

Even in his changed situation, however, he remained very conscious of being a member of the nobility and would not compromise his dignity, even at the cost of losing some excellent opportunities to rid himself of his financial difficulties. Once, famously, he was promised a job as a teacher of Urdu and Persian at Delhi (later St Stephen's) College. All he had to do was appear for an interview with the Principal. Would the Principal come to greet him at the gate?—the poet enquired. When informed that this was not the protocol usually followed between the Principal and the applicants, Ghalib replied, 'I thought this work would enhance my position, not lower it'—and refused to appear for the interview.

The story about the change of his pen name, whether true or fictitious, indicates a similar desire to chalk his own path, and even a certain arrogant awareness of his own unique talents. Once, for example, he composed a tareekh—chronogram—predicting the year of his death. It so happened that a terrible pestilence swept across Delhi that year, killing thousands. Ghalib, his tareekh notwithstanding, survived. Afterwards, always witty and humorous—and self-aware—he wrote that he had stayed in the city while thousands fled or died because he did not wish to die with a crowd.

Altaf Husain Hali, an admirer and disciple of Ghalib's, writes that Ghalib was a very handsome man in his youth. Whether it was his distinguished dress and appearance, his social norms, his views on religion and its rituals and taboos, his thoughts about the socio-political order or, finally, his poetic style, he would always deviate from accepted norms. From drinking wine to shunning the Ramzan fast, from missing the prescribed prayers to his fondness for public gambling and resulting indebtedness, all was a matter of fun and jokes for him—and he would turn any criticism on its head with wit and without bitterness. His repartee was matchless, and rarely did he hold back from responding to any comment about his way of life.

It is not surprising, therefore, that Ghalib united many in criticism of him. He was branded a liar, a friend of the English, a drunkard, a person who cared for his own interests alone. And yet, for all the attacks on him, his fame and popularity kept increasing. His friends and followers proclaimed him large-hearted, a true friend, humane, liberal and generous—a man of great self-respect and values.

Of the attacks upon him, Ghalib once said:

Na sataaish ki tamanna na sala ki perwa
Gar naheen hain mere ashaar mein maani na sahi

Not craving appreciation nor caring for reward;
if my verses have no meaning, so be it.

Actually, like most geniuses, Ghalib was a multifaceted person who understood and accepted life with all its complexities and spun these aspects into his ghazals.

The following verse of Ghalib's may be quoted as a good illustration of Ghalib himself:

Bala-e jaan hai Ghalib us ki har baat
Ebarat kya, esharat kya, ada kya

Everything about him wreaks havoc, Ghalib:
his words, his gestures, his style.

This is so true of Ghalib himself. There are layers of meaning in his works that every generation interprets and appreciates in its own way. From Hali to modern-day critics, everyone reads Ghalib with their own perspective.

Ghalib called himself the nightingale of an unborn garden. As old orders change, however, so new gardens are born. In the decades since Ghalib wrote his verses, an exponential growth of knowledge and awareness of the universe has brought new facts to light, often shattering old values, and questioning old beliefs. Thus, the modern mind and sensibility responds to Ghalib's diction and style more naturally and most positively. He becomes the ultimate poet—and is, today, the most quoted Urdu poet.

Among Ghalib's many idiosyncrasies, one was that he initially adopted a dense and heavily Persianized language. He took pride in it:

Tarz-e Bedil mein rekhta kahna
Asadullah Khan qayamat hai

To write Urdu in the style of Bedil,
Asadullah Khan, that is the zenith.

This was written during a phase when he was being criticized for his obtuse and incomprehensible style; thus the comparison with Abdul Qadir Bedil (*c.* 1642–1720), whose Persian poetry was both renowned and famously difficult to understand. Later, Ghalib changed his style and diction and concentrated on using straightforward, uncomplicated language. Even here, however, the freshness and novelty of his thoughts and imagination, and the breadth and meaning in his ideas and words, stamped Ghalib's ghazals with his unique style.

Given their wildly different temperaments and talents, it was perhaps inevitable that a great rivalry should grow between Ghalib and Zauq—and find a rapt audience. While many fictitious, low-minded bazaar jokes exist on the subject, one entertaining episode occurred during the marriage of the prince, Jawan Bakht.

It is said that Zeenat Mahal, the young and powerful wife of Bahadur Shah and mother of Jawan Bakht, asked Ghalib to write a sehra (a type of wedding poem that describes the sehra, the flowered veil, that bridegrooms wear) for this occasion. Ghalib complied, and ended it thus:

Hum sukhan fahm hain Ghalib ke tarafdar naheen
Dekhein is sehre se badh kar koi kah de sehra

I am a connoisseur of verse, not just taking Ghalib's side,
let us see if anyone recites a sehra better than this sehra.

The maqta was noticed and, eventually, came to the emperor's attention. He pointed it out to Zauq and suggested a sehra from him, too.

Zauq's reply was this maqta:

Jin ko daawa hai sukhan ka ye suna do unko
Dekho is tarh se kahte hain sokahnwar sehra

Tell those who claim to compose good verse,
look this is how masters of verse write sehras.

At this, Ghalib realized he had incurred the displeasure of the emperor, and was compelled to write a long excuse, which he titled 'Maazrat', 'apology'. Characteristically, that was, in itself, a masterly poem, in which he says:

Maqta mein ah pari thee sokhan gastaraana baat
Manzoor is se qata mohabbat naheen mujhe

In a maqta it is customary to praise the verse it ends,
I do not mean by this that I adore my own poems.

It may be of interest to quote one couplet each from the sehras that Ghalib and Zauq, both master versifiers, composed. Both have a similar meaning:

Ghalib writes:

Saat dariya se faraaham kiye honge moti
Tab bana hoga is andaaz ka ghaz bhar sehra

Pearls must have been plucked from seven oceans,
only then could such a yard-long sehra be made.

And Zauq:

Ek guhar bhi nahin, sad kaane guhar mein chora
Tera banvaaya hai le le ke jo gauhar sehra

Not a gem left in a hundred mines,
taken one by one for your yard-long sehra.

As noted above, Ghalib wrote in Persian and Urdu both. In fact, his Persian diwan is much more voluminous and he prized it far more than his Urdu work, calling his Urdu verse 'berang', colourless, when compared to his Persian poetry:

Farsi been taa be beeni naqshhaai rang rang
Beguzaar az majmua-e Urdu ke berange mun ast

Read my Persian verse to see colours of such hue!
Overlook the Urdu writing, which is colourless.

However, ultimately, it is this small Urdu diwan of his that brought Ghalib the universal acclaim and the unrivalled position that he craved then, and enjoys today. It is through his Urdu poetry that he took classical ghazals to new heights, and laid the foundation for modern ghazals. Iqbal, the great poet of the following generation, would write in an elegy on Ghalib:

Fikr-e insaan per teri hasti se yeh roshan hua
Hai par-e murgh-e takhiyul ki rasai ta kujaa

Your being made human thought aware of this—
how far may soar the wings of the mind!

Ghalib may also be called the founder of modern Urdu prose. He was a master prose writer, a diarist and composer of engrossing, intimate letters. Perhaps it would be possible to compile a vivid socio–political history of that period in Delhi just on the basis of Ghalib's diaries and letters.

Ghalib died in the year 1869, in penury and much pain. He had composed the following verse a few days before his death and would often recite it:

Dam-e wapseen ber sare raah hai
Azeezo ab Allah hi Allah hai

The returning breath is on its way now,
dear ones, now Allah and Allah alone.

Momin: Hakeem Momin Khan 'Momin' (1800–1851/52)*

The maqta of a famous ghazal by Hakeem Momin Khan
goes thus:

> *Jise aap ginte thie aashna jise aap kahte thie bewafaa*
> *Main wohee hoon Momin-e mubtala, tumhein yaad ho ke na*
> *yaad ho*

The one you counted an acquaintance, the one you said
was unfaithful,
I am that same afflicted Momin, you may remember
me . . . or not.

One wonders if the last line of his own maqta has become
true for Momin's current predicament. Amongst the top
poets of his time, a master of the craft of the pure ghazal,
a fine lyricist and true gentleman, he seems to have
become rather neglected amidst the new galaxy of poets
being paraded now. With changing times and tastes, the
popularity of Momin has declined and his own line, 'you
may remember me . . . or not' applies to him aptly.

Momin Khan was born in the year 1800. His father
was Hakeem Ghulam Nabi Khan Kashmiri; and hikmat—
or Unani (Greek) medicine—was his family vocation. He
received his early education in Persian and Arabic from

---

* Much of the information and anecdotes about Momin, here, have been
sourced from Muhammad Husain Azad's *Aab-e Hayaat* ('The Water of
Life').

Shah Abdul Qadir (son of Shah Waliullah, a famous Islamic scholar, historiographer, bibliographer and philosopher) and adopted his family profession thereafter.

Momin was an unusually brilliant person. His education was deep and wide. He had a wide exposure to a variety of disciplines and languages including Arabic, Persian and Urdu; medicine, mathematics and astrology. Music and chess were other areas of keen interest that he cultivated with care. However, like many bright persons, Momin Khan was temperamentally mercurial. He could not stick to one vocation and did not practise medicine for long. Instead, he developed other hobbies. He was able to obtain such an expertise in astrology that all the acknowledged masters of the field accepted that he was unparalleled in the skill. There are many interesting anecdotes about how his predictions about various events came to be correct, and how his knowledge, based on precise calculations of the movement of the stars, helped people locate lost articles or solve other kinds of problems.

His own couplet about his knowledge of astrology has a peculiar pathos:

In naseebon per kya akhtar sanaash
Aasmaan bhi kya sitam ijaad hai!

Given this fate and given knowledge of the stars, too—
What cruel ironies the heavens do contrive!

Besides astrology, Momin excelled in chess. There were only one or two professionals in Delhi who could beat him at the game. He was also a master in composing tareekhs and had written the tareekh of his own death—*ba dasto baazoo shikast*, 'with the breaking of hands and feet'. Exactly according to the prediction, he died in 1851/52, falling from the parapet of his terrace.

Momin Khan was very conscious of his self-respect, and unwilling to take even a minor obligation from anyone. He never wrote a qasida for anyone except once, for a nobleman of Patiala, Raja Ajit Singh, who had invited him to the palace in which he was staying during a visit to Delhi. It so happened that Momin was passing along the road on which the raja was staying. When the raja learnt that Momin Khan was passing by, he had him invited, treated him with great respect, and, when it was time for Momin to leave, gave him a cow-elephant.

An interesting story follows. When Momin was to depart, Raja Ajit Singh offered him the cow-elephant to take, and ride home upon. Momin stood up with folded hands and declared that he was a poor man, how would he feed this beast and what would he eat himself? At this, the raja asked that another hundred rupees be given to the poet. Momin rode home upon the animal, but he sold it before it had had its first meal!

Much like Ghalib, Momin had grown up in affluence. His father was among the royal physicians and had a good income from the estate that he had inherited. Momin inherited the estate, too. He also received his share from the pension that his family got from the English in their capacity as hakeems. He lived on this pension in Delhi and did not seek money from other sources. It is said that once he had agreed to go to the Patiala court, where the then maharaja offered him a monthly stipend of a thousand rupees. However, he declined the offer when he learnt that a court singer had been employed at the same salary.

Momin's first—and last—ustad was Shah Naseer but, for most of his writing life, he wrote without a teacher. He had a natural aptitude for poetry and tried his hand at every poetic form: ghazal, qasida, rubayee, masnavi, vasokht, tarkeeb, bund, etc. However, Momin's aesthetic and romantic temperament was best suited to the ghazal; and his ghazals, though broadly confined to subjects of beauty and love, are renowned for their delicacy and fineness of expression, and fanciful yet moving turns of phrase.

Momin may perhaps be called the true romantic poet of Urdu, a poet who portrays romantic love most exquisitely. The amorous disposition in Momin's poetry is also a part of the romance of life. In celebrating romantic love in all its manifestations, he explored the lover's moods and sensualities with purity of diction, deeply nuanced phrases and indirect modes of expression. Sometimes, his verse would also make way for metaphysical expressions of love and the figure of the lover.

Besides his aestheticism, what distinguishes Momin from his contemporaries is how he personalized his subjects, as opposed to objectifying them. Unlike most other poets, Momin is talking *to* the beloved mashooqs of his verse, not *about* them. This gives his subjects an enhanced reality.

His control of the maqta, moreover, is unmatched. The way he is able to play with his pen name and create puns on the word 'momin'—a pious Muslim and often a figure of derision in ghazals—is something to be specially noted. Momin, the lover, the idol worshipper, the wayward, forlorn vagabond, is pitted against the pious man who tries to mislead this footloose enjoyer of a happy life towards the ways of piety. But the essential man, Momin, does not leave his moorings easily, and even in piety finds his own way of life:

> *Zikr-e sharaab-o hur kalam-e khuda mein dekh*
> *Momin main kya kahoon mujhe kya yaad aa gaya*

At the mention of wine and houries in the Quran,
O Momin, what can I say of what all I did recall!

Elsewhere, when Momin goes astray, he sets off for the Kaaba leaving behind the temple and his idols. It is to be noted that this piety of Momin's is mocked. He is described as one who has lost the right path:

> *Allah re gumrahi but-o but-khana chor kar*
> *Momin chala hai kaabe ko ek parsa ke saath*

Allah re, losing his way and leaving the *but-khana*,
Momin goes to Kaaba now in virtuous company.

Or:

Dushman-e Momin rahe yeh but sada
Mujh se mere naam ne yeh kya kiya

Enemies of Momin these *but* have ever been,
O what this name of mine has done to me!

Here the 'buts', idols, are those mashooq, beloved, who are
suspicious of Momin because of his name.

And the final mockery:

Chal diye su-e-Haram, ku-e butaan so Momin
Jab diya ranj buton ne, toh khuda yaad aaya

Momin sets off to Haram from the quarters of the *buts*,
when the *buts* gave him grief, then God came to mind.*

For all Momin's seeming light-heartedness, even disdain
for overt piety, a high spiritual status has also been claimed
for him. A tradition goes that some years after his death,
Nawab Mustafa Khan Shefta, an intimate disciple of
Momin's, had a dream in which an envelope was delivered
to him. The envelope was sealed with the words 'Momin
Jannati', Momin of Heaven. When Shefta opened the
envelope, he found a letter from Momin telling him to
take care of Momin's surviving family, which was facing
hardships. The next day, Shefta sent two hundred rupees
to Momin's house—and soon received a message that the

---

* Haram is also the Kaaba.

money had been needed desperately as the roof of the house was leaking badly.

Momin died in 1851/52 and, apart from his Urdu diwan, he left behind a Persian diwan, and works in prose.

Nawab Mirza Khan Dagh Dehlvi (1831–1905)

Urdu hai jis ka naam hum heen jaante hain Dagh
Sare jahaan mein doom hamaari zubaan ki hai.

I alone know Urdu, O Dagh,
my tongue amazes the world.

So proclaims Dagh, and perhaps not too unjustly. In his time, he was the only star left in the firmament of Urdu poetry, so much so that he was able to say '*Urdu hi woh nahin jo hamari zubaan nahin*'—it isn't Urdu if I don't speak it.

Dagh was born in Delhi in 1831. His father, Nawab Shamsuddin, was hanged by the British on charges of conspiring to murder the then British Resident, William Fraser. To tell this most romantic story in brief: the nawab and Fraser both loved the same woman, the beautiful Wazir Khanam, Dagh's mother; and the nawab had Fraser assassinated. The story is wonderfully told in *Kai Chand thei sar-e Aasman* (translated as *The Mirror of Beauty*) by Shamsur Rahman Faruqi.

Dagh was only about six or seven years old when his father died. Thereafter, his mother married Mirza Fakhru,

one of the sons of Bahadur Shah Zafar. Until the death
of Mirza Fakhru in 1856, Dagh lived in the Red Fort
with his mother, and it was here that he received his
training and education. It was in the sometimes flowery
and classical aesthetic of the Fort that his poetry sprang its
roots, as he passed from the tutelage of Mirza Fakhru to
that of Ustad Zauq. Under Zauq's training, and with his
own hard work and practice, he soon acquired the status
of an ustad himself.

Once the prince died, however, Dagh had to leave the
Fort with his mother, and he went to stay in the city of
Delhi. But the disturbances followed the very next year, in
1857, making life in Delhi extremely precarious, so Dagh
and his family moved to Rampur, where Rampur's nawab
received him with great honour and appointed him the
main companion to his crown prince, Kalb Ali Khan.

Some years later, after the death of Kalb Ali Khan, Dagh
left Rampur for Hyderabad. He was welcomed warmly in
the city and appointed ustad to the nizam of Hyderabad,
Mir Mahboob Ali Khan.

It is here that Dagh died in the year 1905, from an
attack of paralysis; and it is here that he lies buried.

When Dagh began to write, the world of Urdu literature
was very different from that inhabited by his immediate
predecessors. The Mughal court, the great centre of
poetry and art, was no more. Old Delhi itself was in ruins.
Lucknow, another hub of culture, had been annexed by the
British. Only a few provinces like Rampur and Hyderabad
had functional courts of any kind left.

All the old stalwarts of Urdu poetry, too, were long gone, and Dagh had practically no rivals in the art. Unchallenged from any quarter, he could declare:

Naheen khel ayie Dagh yaaron se kah do
Ke aati hai Urdu zubaan aate aate

It is not a joke, tell my friends, O Dagh,
Urdu is only learnt as it comes, by and by.

Dagh may be called the last great poet of the old classical tradition. His poetry is the poetry of playfulness, wantonness and a kind of youthful exuberance. Dagh could mould a ghazal into a form of intimate poetic conversation, while remaining faithful to all its conventions. He introduced common speech into his poetry and combined the poetic manners of the Lucknow and Delhi schools. In its totality, Dagh's poetry is idiomatic and appealing, laden with good humour. He did not take the idea of love to philosophical heights but engaged with the experience of love at a human level, often sensuous or even erotic. He uses the simplest Urdu with great emphasis on idioms, playing wittily with turns of phrase, urbane and light-hearted. When he writes of his mashooq, he appears to be lively and wanton, even naughty.

Here are some examples of his free-flowing style:

Jo tumhari tarh tumse koi jhoothe waade karta
Tum hi munsifi se keh do, tumhen aitbaar hota?

If one made you promises as false as your own,
you be the judge: would you believe a word?

In contrast, Ghalib's couplet on the same theme appears
rather complicated:

Tere vaade par jiye hum to yeh jaan jhoot jaana
Ki khushi se mar na jaate agar aitbaar hota

If you think I lived on your promises, know it's not so:
I would have died of ecstasy had I believed in you.

Back to Dagh:

Jo nigaah ki thi zaalim to phir aankh kyun churaayi?
Wohi teer kyon na maara, jo jigar ke paar hota?

When you have looked at me, *zaalim*, why did you steal
your gaze?
Why not shoot the arrow that would have pierced my
heart?

On this theme, Ghalib writes:

Koi mere dil se pooche, tere teer-e neemkash ko
Yeh khalish kahan se hoti jo jigar ke paar hota

Ask my heart about your arrow half-drawn,
how would I pine if it had pierced through?

Dagh's carefree style embraces all love-related themes. Thus, Dagh writes:

> *Tere vaade ko but-e heela joo, na qaraar hai na qayaam hai*
> *Kabhi shaam hai kabhi subh hai, kabhi subh hai kabhi shaam hai*

> Your promise, deceiving *but*, is inconstant, untrue,
> from morning to eve and back again, without a sign of you.

> *Kaun ghamkhaar ilahi shab-e gham hota hai?*
> *Ab toh pehlu mein mere dard bhi kam hota hai.*

> Who stays by my side in my nights of grief?
> Now even the pain in my side has subsided.

Dagh seems to have done well in Hyderabad, where he was showered with honorifics: Nawab Nizam Jang Bahadur, Sipah Salar, Yar-e Wafadar, Muqrib-us Sultan, Bulbul-e Hindustan, Jahan Ustad—Master-administrator, Commander-in-chief, Loyal friend, Intimate of the Sultan, Nightingale of Hindustan, Teacher of the world . . .

Dagh had many eminent disciples across India. With both Delhi and Lucknow no longer centres, let alone schools, of poetry, Dagh had become an institution in himself. A 'Dagh school' came about. His disciples include some famous poets of the future (for example, Jigar Muradabadi, Seemab Akbarabadi, Mubarak Azimabadi, Nooh Narvi, and many more), who would all acknowledge their debt to their ustad, proudly proclaiming that they were from the Dagh school.

The most famous of them, Muhammad Iqbal, became one of the greatest poets of all time, though of a different type, and composed an elegy on Dagh that describes Dagh's style most elegantly and perhaps most appropriately. Some of the lines from his elegy are:

Utthen-ge Azar hazaron sher ke but-khaane se
Maye pilayen-ge naye saqi naye paimane se
Likhkhi jayengi kitab-e dil ki tafseeren bahut
Hongi aye khwab-e jawaani teri taabeerien bahut
Hu bahu khechegaa leqin ishq ki tasweer kaun
Uth gaya nabak fagan maarega dil per teer kaun.

Many new Azars will arise from the *but-khana* of verse,*
new *saqis* will come to serve wine in new goblets,
treatises on the book of the heart will be written,
O dreams of youth, you shall have many visions—
but who will now draw the picture of *ishq* so well!
Gone is the master archer, who will now pierce the heart
with arrows!

---

* Azar is the father of Abraham. The latter is extolled in the Quran and the Bible for his unwavering belief in God, at whose command Abraham was even willing to sacrifice his own son. Azar, on the other hand, was a maker of idols. Unsurprisingly, father and son had a contentious relationship; Abraham destroyed Azar's workshop. In this verse, the mention of Azar and the 'but-khana' of verse implies that poetry, too, is an idol-house—in a positive sense.

Apart from his four diwans, Dagh has left behind a masnavi, a few qasidas and rubayees, a bunch of letters and a long narrative poem on the destruction of Delhi.

My Little Story

The story of my coming across this book may be of some interest. I had completed my matriculation examination with science subjects, which was in vogue those days, though I never seemed to be on a good wicket there. During the three months' vacation after the exams, my father asked me to visit the Government Urdu Library in Patna, a ten-minute walk from our house. In those days, during the late 1950s, the library, like all government establishments, was functional. Amongst the books he wanted me to read was Mirza Farhatullah Baig's *Dilli ki Aakhri Shama*.

After my retirement from a long career in banking, I thought of translating some gems of Urdu literature produced in the not-too-distant past that seem to be lost to the present generation. That distant memory of my time in the Urdu library came back to me then. Today, we are witnessing, perhaps, a revival of interest in Urdu poetry. In addition, Baig's book is a cultural portrait of a period of Delhi that, although not too distant, has long been fading from public memory. It may interest modern readers to experience a glimpse of this part of Delhi's past.

When I started on this book, I felt I did not have the capability and stamina to complete it alone. For that I sought the help of my young friend, Parvati Sharma, and invited her to be the co-author with me for this project. I would request her to add her own foreword to this introduction where she may like to highlight some other special features of this work.

An Accidental Translator by Parvati Sharma

It was sometime in 2014 that Mr Sulaiman Ahmad, whom I call Mani Ammun, suggested the idea of our collaborating on this translation of *Dilli ki Aakhri Shama*. I cannot read Urdu, I have never translated prose, let alone poetry, and I did not know of Farahtullah Baig's work. In that sense, I was more the project's intended audience than a potential collaborator. When I read Mani Ammun's translation of the book, however, I was immediately taken by Baig's wry and conversational tone and was attracted by the challenge of trying to capture the nuances of Urdu verse in English.

No two languages are as different, perhaps: Urdu's formal subtleties and grand imagery is a world apart from the relative directness, indeed sparseness, of the English tongue; and the ghazal, with its fractured yet multiple meanings, almost defies translation.

Over the past seven years, over long conversations, over many meals and cups of tea, Mani Ammun decoded these nuances for me. My 'work', such as it is, was more that of a pupil than a co-translator. Even now, as we reach the end of this long journey, I cannot claim to have fully understood the many layers of meaning that fill the ghazals in this book.

Perhaps, on the other hand, I have come to appreciate the underlying sentiment of this work and the poetry that fills it. It is the ache of nostalgia; the hearkening for a warmth and light that is both so close and familiar, and yet forever gone.

It is a nostalgia that may resonate with new meaning for Baig's readers today. In 2021, as this book prepares to go to press, we, too, remember better times: times in which autocracies were not on the rise across the world, times in which a pandemic had not imbued every human interaction with anxiety, times in which 'climate emergency' and 'ecological disaster' were terms reserved for dystopian fiction.

Milan Kundera, the exiled Czech writer whose work so often addresses the idea of nostalgia, once wrote that 'The struggle of man against power is the struggle of memory against forgetting.' In the epilogue to Baig's book, his fictional narrator, Karimuddin, suggests that his carefully gathered account of Delhi's last great mushaira may never get published—that his manuscript will be lost, much like the world it evokes. But that is not what happened. Not only was Baig's book published, it remains one of the classics of modern Urdu literature, holding in its few pages a gift: of remembrance.

Notes on the Text

A Note on Some Conventions and Tropes in the Ghazal

In the universe of the ghazal, a number of words are employed quite frequently. Their connotations extend far beyond their definitions. It may be correct to say that the great ghazal poets' usage of many such words gives their work multilayered meanings, which can keep changing depending upon the context and time.

Person/gender

The beloved/subject of a ghazal is often addressed in the masculine gender. This is partly a result of the fact that Persian, from which language the ghazal is derived, is gender-neutral, unlike Urdu. Moreover, the cultural milieu of the ghazal's evolution in India was such that the beloved would, in those times, be pardah-nasheen, that is, veiled—and it would have been a breach of social etiquette to then describe her in 'public'. (It may be worth noting in this context that photography was long considered violative of such modesty.)

Women poets (ghazalgo, those who compose ghazals) would also give themselves a takhallus (pen name), which would not indicate their gender. Often, the takhallus was Makhfi—'hidden'—it was used by Emperor Aurangzeb's daughter, Zeb-un-Nissa.

Gender neutral subjects allowed poets a wide scope to express ideas beyond the confines of the traditional mashooq. For instance, a gender-free mashooq could include themes such as maarfat (reaching the sublime), rebellion, etc.

It is worth noting that, before the ghazal came to be developed in proper Urdu diction, an earlier form was being practised in what was called the Deccan. While Urdu was evolving under the influence of the Mughal court and tending to be more Persianized, the same language was being used in the Deccan, perhaps in a less sophisticated way, and was termed Deccani. Here, the love for the mashooq was expressed in gendered terms. Wali Deccani was an important poet of this time, and was recognized as such by Dilliwallas when he came and lived in Delhi.

Ishq

Literally romantic love but also used metaphorically to allude to love for God. Ishq can also refer to a cause, be it a struggle against tyranny, a noble project of service to humanity or emphasis on moral values.

Mashooq, Mahbub, But, Zaalim, Qatil, Sitamgar, Sitamju, Kaafir, Sanam, Parda-nashin, Fitnagar, Yaar, Ishwagar (pronouns such as us, un, woh, tum, etc. are also used to refer to this person)

All are terms for the beloved, with a vast variety of connotations. The beloved does not just embody fascination or longing, but can imply a passion for unification with the divine, a quest for nature and its beauties or a desired social, political and just order.

Since the dramatic conceit of a ghazal often hinges on the unattainability of the mashooq and all he embodies, the many synonyms for 'beloved' play upon the idea of the poet's constant rejection. Thus, zaalim or qatil—a tyrant, an executioner; sitamgar—one who inflicts cruelty; fitnagar—one who brings about disorder. Sanam and but both call upon the beloved as an 'idol', beautiful yet indecipherable. 'But' connotes both beauty and wisdom, and may have been derived from 'Buddha'. The 'idol-house', but-khaana or sanam-khaana, is where the poet goes and is unrequited. Kaafir is one who denies the truth: the truth of the poet's love.

Modern ghazals often use the term ironically; mashooq symbolizing the person or system that oppresses the people for whom the poet speaks.

Hijr, firaaq, judaai

Separation from the beloved, and thus also the non-achievement of all those longings and ideals that the beloved represents.

Visaal

Meeting, or unification. The word is just the opposite of hijr and connotes not only meeting the beloved but also the fulfilment of all the poet's desires, ideals or ambitions.

Raqeeb, ghair, doosra, odoo

Most translations of Urdu poetry translate raqeeb as 'rival'. No doubt, the raqeeb is basically the romantic rival of the poet. But in the lexicon of Urdu poetry, he is much more. A villain all right, but also one who becomes quite a sympathetic figure, colourful and even lovable. The story of the poet as a lover cannot be complete without him. It is through him that the beloved tortures the poet, dispensing favours to the raqeeb to make his lover jealous, etc. Also, the poet turns to the raqeeb when he is lonely and needs company for his drinking bouts, or if he wants to reminisce about his old love, as only the raqeeb (the poet's companion throughout the poet's passion for the mashooq) remembers that beauty.

The opening lines of a famous poem by Faiz go thus:

Aa ke waabistaa hain us husn ki yaadein tujh se,
Jis ne is dil ko parikhaana banaa rakhkhaa thaa

Come (o *raqeeeb*) as the memoris of that beauty are associated with you,
which had turned this heart into a dwelling of fairies.

As the story of Adam would not be complete without Satan, the poet's love would be colourless without the raqeeb. He becomes the poet's alter ego.

Ghalib in his inimitable style says:

Raat ke waqt maye piye, saath raqeeb ko liye
Aaye woh yaan khuda kare per na khuda kare ke yun

In the night drunk with wine, having raqeeb for company,
I wish to God he came, but not when in this state I am.

Zaahid, sheikh, pir, maulvi, mullaa, momin

The pious; often holier-than-thou. Such a person is usually perceived as a charlatan, a pretentious deceiver instead of a person of true piety. Such negative connotations may have their origins in Persian ghazals, which had a great influence on their Indian counterparts. Over its history, Persia (and some other Muslim societies) witnessed an increasing concentration of political power in its religious seminaries, leading to a nexus between political power and the clergy. Religious doctrine, interpretation and discourse became ritualistic, dogmatic and prejudiced. Persian poets expressed criticism of such developments through the images and symbols in their ghazals.

Thus, along with zaahid or sheikh, the places and culture associated with such men, like the masjid and Kaaba, or even being a Musalmaan, were represented as symbols of decadence and came to be ridiculed. Naturally, their antitheses, temples and idols, taverns and wine-drinking, were eulogized—one of the reasons why the beloved is called 'sanam', 'but' or 'kaafir'. These latter tropes represented an open mind and free, unsuppressed human will.

Saqi, peer-e moghan

The literal meaning of saqi is 'cup-bearer' or 'dispenser of drinks'—a modern-day equivalent of a bartender or tavern-keeper. Earlier English translators, less familiar with the temperament, ambience and nuances of Persian or Urdu ghazals, often mistranslated it as 'butler'.

As with all the other tropes, the connotations are aplenty. In a straightforward verse, saqi serves wine to the poet and his companions when they are out for a night of enjoyment, perhaps escaping from a masjid. Better still would be if the mashooq could be around and the ubiquitous raqeeb kept out.

The same saqi, however, can also be the provider of the wine of gnosis to devotees who want to quench their thirst for divine mysteries. Here, the saqi is a spiritual mentor, the pir, the sufi saint, the spiritual guru.

When a ghazal takes political or social overtones, the saqi may also head the system or the order being protested. Here, the saqi assumes the role of the unjust tyrant who rules in an unfair, biased and prejudiced manner. In such symbolism, the saqi may be an unfair distributor of wine—partial to the raqeeb and inconsiderate to the lover, averse to giving him wine liberally.

Daaman

The lower part of a kurta or shirt, worn both by the lover and the beloved. Daaman is used in different ways; for instance, daaman kheenchna is to beseech the beloved by tugging at his hem; daaman chaak karna is the poet tearing his own clothes in his frenzy. Daaman tar is to indulge in sin—an allusion to lovemaking, etc.

A Note on Clothing

Readers will notice that Baig expends great effort in describing the clothing and mannerisms of his characters. Not only does this help to create the 'snapshots' or 'portraits' he set out to do, it also brings alive the particular formality of that age. As Baig writes in a footnote to his book: 'In this time, gentlemen dressed fully even while at home.' Visits to the zenana, the women's quarters, were formally arranged, and most of the day was spent in the mardana, the men's area. Visitors would arrive, sit in the respectful dozanoo posture—that is, on one's knees—and discuss various matters. 'There was little idle time,' writes Baig, and the air was formal 'as people would be light-hearted only with very close friends . . . Laughing or talking loudly was considered bad manners.'

Baig also has a long and detailed footnote on the various kinds of dresses, from hats to pyjamas, favoured at the time. Of headgear, he writes that the 'chogoshia topi' was common in town. A round, raised hat with four prominent seams, dividing the hat into four 'sections', the chogoshia topi could be 'worn in different ways', by raising or lowering the height of its brim, for example, or by wearing it raised or flattened upon the head. The four seams might also be expanded to five or even eight. If there were five seams, writes Baig, each would be cut to resemble the 'parapets of a city or fort boundary wall'. A five-seamed, or panchgoshia topi, would be worn after having it moulded upon a frame, at which, writes Baig, 'it looks like the dome of Humayun's tomb'. A man who favoured an eight-seamed version would flatten the hat so much that it would 'expand into the shape of a lotus'. This variation of the topi was often worn at an angle. The hat's brim would be decorated with lace. Famously, Bahadur Shah Zafar wore a chogoshia hat, though in his case it was decorated with elaborate embroidery and 'a profusion of pearls and gems'.

Two other popular styles of headgear were the arkhcheen and the dopalli topis. The former was embroidered with brocade lace, while the latter was simpler: an oval hat made with two pieces of cloth, resembling a skullcap. Styles of wearing the dopalli varied from Delhi to Lucknow, writes Baig: 'The Delhi cap is big enough to cover the entire head, whereas the Lucknow one just perches on the hair.'

Only Ghalib, as Baig notes, wore a distinctively tall fur hat.

Almost every man in Baig's narrative wears an angarkha, a kurta-like shirt with as many variations as its wearers. 'Because everyone is fond of exercise,' wrote Baig, those who wished to show off their physiques would have the sleeves stitched tight, or roll them up. Some might wear a kurta under the angarkha, but this was rare. Men from the Fort favoured a kaftan robe (called a sherwani outside the Fort) of velvet or jamawar weave (embroidered wool and silk). The kaftan's borders might be decorated with lace or, for the 'very stylish', with sable fur. No buttons were used, only cord knobs and eyelets, romantically named 'ashiq-o mashooq', the lover and the beloved.

Those who did not wear a robe over their angarkha might drape a large shawl or shoulder-mantle 'folded into the shape of a samosa' on their backs. A rare few used this cloth as a waistband.

Next, the pyjama, 'always of expensive cloth', writes Baig, such as gulbadan, mashroo, ghalta or atlas—all exquisite varieties of silk. The one-bar pyjama ('bar' being a measure of width) was preferred, but narrower cuts were coming into fashion.

On their feet, men wore jootis, in which department the salimshahi style—with a narrow heel—was becoming fashionable, though an older style called ghetli still survived.

The men were not only careful about their clothes, but also their appearance. Baig writes that bodybuilding was 'a popular hobby in the city'. Hardly anyone would step out of the house without a bamboo stick—procured with much effort, 'soaked with oil, rubbed with henna, and then hung in the kitchen'. After a while, the bamboo's colour turned black and its weight increased so 'it appears to have been fused with lead'. Its owner would now take it out, 'walking with a swagger'. Few among the elite were not trained in some form of martial skill, such as 'bunk', 'banot' and 'lakri'. 'These are considered to be signs of nobility.'

Some terms related to clothing that occur in the book, and Baig does not elaborate upon, are described below:

Achkan: a jacket or robe, similar to the sherwani

Angocha: gamcha; a large towel-like cloth; generally used by Hindus

Banat: decorative work on cloth, similar to gota work (appliqué embroidery)

Bar: the breadth of cloth; pyjamas narrowed by one fold would be 'one-bar pyjamas'

Chogha: robe

Choli: a shirt. Neechi or Unchi choli would refer to how low or high it was cut

Doshala, shali kerchief: a kind of shawl or shoulder-mantle

Gulbadan: a type of striped silk

Gulshan: a brand of that time

Jamawar, Kamkhab: were (and are) weaves worn on special occasions. What is now called 'paisley' was a design widely used in Persia and incorporated into these weaves. Kamkhab was woven using a mixture of silk and gold or silver thread, and jamawar with silk and wool

Karchobi: a specific type of zari embroidery that results in a more pronounced pattern

Khirkidar: high turban

Nefa: the part of a pyjama where the string runs

Papakh: a large fur hat particular to Russia, the Caucasus and central Asia

Pashmina: a particular type of very soft wool, particular to Kashmir. Shatoosh is a more expensive and exclusive subtype of pashmina

Saslet: colourful silk

Soozni: a less elaborate form of embroidery; functional and comfortable

Zari: embroidery with gold or silver thread, or even gems

A Note on Complexion

While Baig paints his detailed portraits of the life and times of poets in the golden age of Urdu poetry in Delhi, he also sheds unexpected light on how colour and complexion may be described so differently across languages. In Urdu, for example, a man's face might have a 'sabz'—literally greenish—tinge. In English, of course, a green face would suggest either literal indigestion or metaphorical envy; in Urdu, however, it only means that the man sported a stubble, a five o'clock shadow. Thus:

Champai: like the champa flower, similar to the magnolia; the colour would be a kind of pale off-white.

Missi: red lead powder used to darken the teeth or lips; a popular form of make-up for men and women

Paan ka lakha: the colour of the juice of paan; for habitual eaters of paan, it would leave a slight stain on the lips.

Sabz: green. Of a complexion, indicates the hint of a
    stubble or five o'clock shadow (thus, 'sabz jhalakti hui',
    reflecting green)
Sharbati: a pale yellowish-orange, used to describe the
    colour of one's eyes, and to suggest a beguiling quality
    in the gaze. In cloth, it indicates a pastel colour.
Surkh: red, ruddy

Glossary

Aadab, salaam: respectful greetings

Chobdar: herald

Hakeem: physician

Haveli: a large house. At the time of which Baig writes, 'haveli' was also used as an ironic diminutive for the Red Fort

Hazrat: often placed before an august name or honorific; like 'the Hon'ble'

Hikmat or Unani medicine: A system of medicine that was brought to India by the Arabs, who remained faithful to its source, giving it the name Unani ('of Greece')

Insha-Allah: God-willing

Khuda hafiz: God keep you safe

Maqta: the last couplet of a ghazal, in which the poet usually includes his pen name

Mardana: men's quarters

Masnavi: a type of narrative poem written in rhyming couplets, with internally rhyming lines. Subjets can vary from Rumi's philosophical treatise on Islamic mysticism to the nineteenth-century Lucknow poet Mir Hasan's love story

Matla: the first couplet of a ghazal

Maulvi, Mullah: religious scholar of Islam; theologian well versed in Islam and Islamic law and a scholar who would command a certain respect in society; Muslim priest

Mian: used to address a young man of good lineage

Mirza: prince, young nobleman

Misra: a line of poetry

Morchal: a peacock-feather whisk

Mushaira: a symposium of poets

Qafia: the rhyme-scheme of a ghazal

Qasida: ode

Radeef: the last word of every couplet in a ghazal, which is repeated throughout the poem

Rubayee: quatrain

Shamiana: a canopy used on ceremonial occasions

Sher: a couplet

Takhallus: pen name

Ustad: A mentor, teacher; an acknowledged master of a skill; one who refines the verse of his shagird (disciple)

Zenana: women's quarters

Titles of the Emperor and Other Royalty

Badshah Salamat: the king, who may live

Hazrat Peer-o Murshid: revered elderly mentor, a spiritual guide. Here, it implies the king.

Hazrat Zill-e Elahi: revered shadow of the Glorified

Hazrat Zillulah: shadow of the Lord

Huzoor-e Wala: exalted huzoor

Huzoor: sire

Jahan Panah: protector of the world

Mumlika-o Saltanata: the sultanate of God's world

Peshgah-i Aali: the highest place for submitting a request

Qibla-e Alam: the prayer direction of the world. Qibla is Kaaba, facing which Muslims offer prayers. A title of respect for a very venerable person (also used for Mirza Fakhru)

Saheb-e Alam-o Alammian Hazrat: Master of this world and of all worlds

Waliahad Bahadur: heir apparent

Zill-e Subhani: Shadow of the Almighty

The Last Light of Delhi

Tamheed

A Beginning

Naam-e nek-e raftagaan zaayaa makun
Taa ba maanad nam-e nekat barkaraar

Do not let the repute of your elders perish,
so that your good name, too, does last.

The late Ghalib would say that man is a vortex of ideas—but for these ideas to churn, some external trigger is essential. The human mind is a storehouse of inspiration but, to open this treasury, you need a key. I have been interested in reading and hearing about the lives of Urdu poets since I was a child, but there was never any catalyst to inspire me to gather these details in one place, in such a way that these musings, in the form of words, would become a pleasing motion picture.

When a thing is to happen, its reasons emerge on their own. You see, it so happened that I came across a portrait of Hakeem Momin Khan Momin Dehlvi in a pile of old papers. The moment I saw the portrait, the idea came to me: 'You too set up a mushaira like that assembly of poets in the late Mohammad Husain Azad's *Nairang-iye Khayal*; but instead of offering commentaries on their works, just reveal them in pictures that come alive.'

The idea took root, and grew to give the mushaira a broad outline. But one thing I wasn't sure of: how to gather poets from different ages in one place? This couplet by the late Amirullah Tasleem unravelled the knot:

Jawaani se zeyaada waqt-e peeri josh hotaa hai,
Bhadaktaa hai chiraag-e subh jab khaamosh hota hai

There is greater fervour in old age than in youth;
the flame burns brightest before it is put out.

The couplet brought the very last age of Delhi's poets before my eyes—and I became convinced, in my heart, that instead of all the poets of Urdu, I might make a sketch of this last era of Delhi.

It is believed that a patient recovers briefly before he perishes. So, as far as Urdu poetry is concerned, Bahadur Shah Sani's[*] rule was such a period of recovery for Delhi. His kingship was only in name. The salary he received was barely enough to cover the cost of maintaining his Fort. In contrast, a Ganga of wealth flowed through Awadh

---

[*] Bahadur Shah the Second, that is. The first Bahadur Shah ruled very briefly in the early eighteenth century.

and the Deccan. And yet, the bright sands of the banks of the Jamuna remained attractive in the eyes of the people of Delhi. And in this despoiled land, not only poets but such masters of every art and skill assembled that it would be difficult to find their like, leave alone in Hindustan but across the world.

Times do not remain unchanged. Even before 1857, many of these masters had already departed this world. The few who remained were scattered helter-skelter by the storms of the Ghadar.* Each one sought refuge wherever he thought he might be provided for. Hyderabad and Rampur flourished as Delhi was abandoned. Many of the nobility left their houses in such a way that they would never see Delhi again. The few who are left behind are ready to take their leave. Many have passed away, and many pass away by the day. A day will come when no one will be able to tell you where Momin lived, just as no one except me, perhaps, knows where he is buried.

Thinking of these fading lights, the idea came to me, bolstered by that portrait of Momin Khan, that I might light such a lamp for Urdu, in the light of which people of future generations would be able to make out the faces of these benefactors of the language, even if they appear a little dim and blurred. When reading their works, a sketch of their features, no matter how vague, might come before their

---

* The events of 1857 were termed a 'mutiny' by the British and India's 'first war of Independence' by later nationalist historians. Nowadays, the events are usually termed the 'Uprising'; and, at the time, they were referred to as 'Ghadar'—'unrest'.

eyes. Besides, people of literary taste would appreciate that, when reading a poet's work, if one also has a sense of his features, his manners, the tenor of his voice and the style of his recitation, his temperament and especially his clothes and their style, then his verses have a more distinctive effect, and the pleasure of reading them is doubled. Without some sense of an author's background, reading his work makes no more impression than hearing him on a gramophone record. This is precisely why no work is published these days, in the civilized world, without a preface on the author's life and the circumstances in which the work was written.

These were the thoughts that prompted me to write these few pages.

You will see many photographs in this album that were shot by those masters of the craft themselves; many drawings that are the works of other painters; and many others that are based on photos or sketches, taken down in words. Yet others are scenes that I have drawn based on interviews with the elderly. In every case, however, I have given more weightage to a statement that has been rejected than to one that has been confirmed. By this I mean that if I found even a single statement contradicting some fact or event, I dropped it altogether.

If so many profiles were gathered in one place, surely this work would have become something like an army's dull and colourless register of faces. But here it was that, on the one hand, the late Azad's *Nairang-iye Khayal* gave me the idea of a mushaira, and on the other, Karimuddin Maghfoor's *Tabqat-e Shoara-e Hind* ('Biographies of the Poets of Hindustan') gave me information about a mushaira held in Rajab 1261 [July–August 1845]. Now what? I blended the two and made an outline. This left the colouring that I shall complete myself—albeit, I do not take any responsibility for how badly or well!

I could have written an account of 1261 as if these events occurred before my eyes—and:

Humchu sabza barha royeeda um
Haft sud haftaad Qalib deeda um

(a Persian couplet that translates roughly to mean: Not seven but seventy times have I seen my heart soar, just as greenery grows and rises repeatedly)

Keeping this in mind, I could have made myself a Mirza Saheb of that time. But my conscience would not let me wear the crown of Karimuddin Marhoom's successes on my own head, and throw him out like a fly from the milk*—the very man who played such a major role in the mushaira, in whose house the mushaira was held, who was the moving force behind it. Of course, it is true that his gathering was quite small, and I gave it a vast expanse, bringing almost all the major poets of that period to sit in it.

Now, it is up to the reader to declare whether I succeeded or not. If yes, that is my luck, and my labour

---

* That is, deny him his due. See the footnote on page xxiii for a more detailed explanation of the idiom.

has paid off. If not, please grant me at least this much: that Mirza Saheb had a good idea, which he could not sustain; and what he could not do, we shall achieve. It is possible that someone blessed with talent will prepare a portrait of these giants sleeping in the dust that will be worthy of adorning the world of Urdu.

Here, now, I appear in the garb of Maulvi Karimuddin, but I do say this, that since I'm offering all my hard work to Maulvi Karimuddin, whatever good or bad you may have to say about this book, don't say it to me—say it to Maulvi Saheb, and say it to your heart's content. I will be happy, and my God too!

Was-salaam,
Mirza Farhatullah Baig

Tadbeer

Attempt

Hawas ko hai nishaat-e kaar kya kya
Na ho marnaa to jeenay kaa mazaa kya?

For indulgent desire such passion exists,
If there is no death, what joy does life give?

Karimuddin has come to Delhi from Panipat, determined to acquire an education and make a living. In pursuit of these two ends, he enrols in Delhi College and buys a printing press. Like publishers before and since, Karimuddin realizes that there is little profit in publishing if he doesn't have a bestseller. So, he decides to hold a grand mushaira, a recital featuring the most sought-after poets of Delhi, and publish an account of it—a sure-shot hit. Arranging a mushaira is no small matter, however. The poets of Delhi are talented but also temperamental; the only way to make them attend is to have the emperor's backing. So, a trembling Karimuddin makes his way into the opulent Red Fort to meet the last Mughal who has ever lived in it, Bahadur Shah Zafar.

9

The ageing monarch, a notable poet himself, gives Karimuddin's plan his permission. Relieved, the young publisher hurries to the homes of some legendary masters of the ghazal, Zauq, Momin and Ghalib, to invite them to read at his recital. Somehow or the other, things fall into place. A mushaira will be held in nine days.

My name is Karimuddin and I am from Panipat, a town about forty kos, say eighty kilometres, from Delhi and distinguished in history for its battles.

I have a fairly prosperous ancestry. We were a family of maulvis, but changing times crushed us so that we were reduced to our last pennies. All our property was confiscated.

My father's father then installed himself in a mosque, where he spent his days invoking Allah. Indeed, when investigations into the confiscated property began, he was so overwhelmed by his trust in Allah that he left his affairs entirely in His hands. He did not budge from where he sat. As a result, he lost the means of earning his daily bread.

My father, the late Sirajuddin, unable to face the situation, saved face by holding on to his piety and took to the mosque with such determination that only death made him leave it.

I was born in the year 1337 Hijri, on the day of Eid-ul-Fitr, in June 1919, and received my education from these very elders. However, my restless nature and family disputes finally compelled me to leave Panipat.

In those days, Delhi was acclaimed as a seat of learning. Every kind of scholar filled the city, every stream of scholarship and culture flowed through it. As a mullah makes unswervingly for the mosque, so I left Panipat for Delhi.

The city had only newly acquired printing presses. I would spend the day making a living from copywriting, but even after such laborious work, my thirst for knowledge would take me to scholarly circles.

Delhi College was then newly founded and in search of students, so I too, at the age of eighteen, enrolled myself. I even got a stipend of sixteen rupees, and in this way I was able to quench my thirst for learning to a great extent.

But this was not an age when knowledge was acquired for its own sake. Alongside, now, a means of livelihood had become necessary. So, together with a few friends, I opened a printing press. We rented the haveli of Mubarak-un-nissa Begum in Qazi ke Hauz*, and published translations of well-known Arabic books. But the press did not run as one might have hoped.

This was a time when the craze for Urdu poetry was at its peak; from emperors to ascetics, in this regard, all were cut from the same cloth. It occurred to me that I might

---

* Qazi ke Hauz, now better known as Hauz Qazi, is an area in Old Delhi, distinguished by a beautiful red mosque built by Mubarak Begum, whose own life would well be worth a book of its own. The begum began her life as a dancing girl in Pune. She came to Delhi where she met and married its first British resident, David Ochterlony (1758-1825), during which time she built the mosque still known by her name. After Ochterlony's demise, the begum married a soldier, and fought against the British in the Uprising of 1857. Ambitious women often attract opprobrium, so did the begum; her mosque was nicknamed 'Randi ki Masjid', the whore's mosque. In July 2020, the central dome of the elegant red structure collapsed in heavy rain.

organize a mushaira and publish an account of the life and works of poets based upon it. Perhaps, this might get the press going.

I was never fond of poetry, nor am I now; in fact, I consider its pursuit unworthy, as poetry is not a vocation for the scholarly. Only those who are free of economic worry indulge in it, for their own recreation, and to express their passions.

Myself, I am a man of letters. So were my father and his forefathers. Ordinarily, I would not have dreamt of such worthless frivolity, but what could I do? Necessity bore down heavily upon us, and compelled me to organize the mushaira.

But the problem was, for one thing, that no one will touch you if you are poor in this city, and certainly not if you are poor and unknown; and second, that the only people I knew were maulvis, and what good could they possibly do me in this matter?

After much reflection, I thought of Nawab Zain-ul-Abdeen Khan *Arif*. I had met him a few times. He is a man of delightful disposition. He has a haveli near Lal Kuan, which is also sometimes called a madarsa, in which he lives. Aged about thirty, he is fair-complexioned, tall and well-dressed, though his beard hasn't grown very full: he has just the few stray hairs on his chin. He is both Ghalib's nephew and his disciple, and has taken some tutelage from Shah Naseer, too.

Be that as it may, it was his affection, his gentleness, and most of all his influence that propelled me to approach him and seek his support in my venture.

Early one morning, I left home and arrived at his house, only to learn that he had gone to call upon Hakeem Ahasanullah Khan Saheb, the Prime Minister. Hakeem Saheb's house was in Sirkiwalan.* I retraced my steps and, when I stopped and enquired at *his* house, I learnt that Nawab Zain-ul-Abdeen Khan was within. I sent an entreaty through the chobdar, the herald, and was invited in.

It was a most resplendent house. There is a canal in the courtyard, and a large platform in front, on which stand large-pillared halls, open on all four sides, one after the other. Opulence drips from everything in it.

Before me, reclining upon a bolster, sat Nawab Saheb. I didn't even recognize him: he had shrivelled like a dry leaf, and his face was lined with wrinkles.

I greeted him with a salaam and asked after his well-being.

'What can I say Maulvi Saheb?' he began to reply. 'It is as if my heart is sinking, apparently without cause or disease. I am being treated, but to no avail. Bhai, the time has come for me to make my departure. I am to take the air of this world for just another few days. But tell me, how is it that you have ventured this way today?'

I told him of my circumstances and laid bare my need before him. He pondered a while and then, with a deep sigh, he said, 'Mian Karimuddin, you have hit upon a good

---

* A sirki is a screen made of bamboo. The lane so named must have once been occupied by people engaged in that trade. It is only a few minutes' walk from Lal Kuan.

idea but it will be difficult to execute, my friend. You do not know what manner of animosities have splintered hearts in Delhi's earlier mushairas. My own heart wishes to see such a mushaira, indeed, as I die—in which this city's masters come together. But I do not see the bud of this thought ever flowering. Well, do try, and so shall I. It's possible something may come of it.

'Wait, yes! Let Hakeem Saheb come; a plan has occurred to me. If it works, my last wish shall be fulfilled, and your work will get done, too.'

We were talking thus when Hakeem Saheb came out. A clear and fair-complexioned man, with a thick white beard and a round face marked with a few scars from the pox. His eyes shine with the agility of his mind. He was dressed in white from head to toe. He is a master of hikmat, Unani medicine, and a great scholar of history.

I offered the most respectful greetings. He looked at me with a smile and asked Nawab Saheb, 'This gentleman?'

'One of my old acquaintances,' he replied, 'not a poet himself, but appreciates poetry. These days he's thinking of writing an account of the poets of Delhi, with descriptions of their appearance and examples of their work. He has come to consult me. You know how I am in love with such things. Now, in my last days, my heart yearns to witness one more mushaira of the old style. With your help, the problem may be easily resolved.'

Hakeem Saheb said, 'Mian Arif, do not speak so despondently for God's sake! You are still young. Insha-Allah, your constitution alone shall overcome the disease. And what disease, after all, do you have? Just misgivings! But yes, tell me: what kind of help do you want from me?'

Nawab Saheb said, 'Hakeem ji, only this: get Mian Karimuddin an audience in the royal chambers of the Jahan Panah. I would have gone myself, but do not have the strength. I shall explain everything to him [that is, to Mian Karimuddin]. If Hazrat Zill-e Elahi consents to send his verses, there should be no problem in getting the mushaira going. If, by some misfortune, he refuses, then even thinking of a mushaira is futile. As for the mushaira's various arrangements, I shall take care of those personally, for what will this hapless gentleman understand of such things?'

Hakeem Saheb thought a while about this, then he said, 'Arif, for you I am willing to do anything, so I shall do even more than you ask. Besides, with this, your spirits may be soothed, and the fear of ill-health may leave your heart.

'I cannot speak to Badshah Salamat; but, yes, I shall introduce your friend to Saheb-e Alam,* the prince, Mirza Fath-ul Mulk Bahadur. He's been hankering after a mushaira and has proposed it to Huzoor several times, though Huzoor has deferred the matter. If this gentleman pushes his case with even the slightest force, I am sure Saheb-e Alam will cajole and coax and gain permission.

---

* Fath-ul Mulk Bahadur (c. 1816/18–1856), also known as Mirza Fakhru, was Bahadur Shah Zafar's second son, declared heir-apparent in 1853. Like his father, the prince was a poet, writing under the pseudonym Ramz. At this time, however, it was an elder prince, Muhammad Dara Bakht, who was in line for the throne.

'All right, Maulvi Saheb. Come to the Royal Fort tomorrow at one o'clock. Let me tell the chobdar, he will bring you in. Thereafter, it is up to you and your luck.'

With these words, Hakeem Saheb called for Khuda Baksh. When he came, he told him, 'At one o'clock tomorrow, this gentleman will come to the Haveli.* Bring him to my room.'

Having said this, he turned his attention to Nawab Saheb once again, and I paid my respects and came away.

The next day, at one o'clock, with all the dignity of a maulvi, fitted with gown and turban, I reached the royal court. Khuda Baksh was waiting by the Lahori Darwaza. He took me to Hakeem Saheb's sitting room, or what used to be called the nashist. It was next to the Diwan-e Aam.†
Hakeem Saheb was seated within, writing something. He looked up at me and said, 'Aji Maulvi Saheb, I have done your work! It so happened that I met Saheb-e Alam Mirza Fath-ul Mulk Bahadur this very morning. He was delighted with this proposal, and declared, "I shall go and get Jahan Panah's permission, but the arrangements for this mushaira should be such that we, too, may attend!" But sit—it may be that you are summoned any minute.'

I had just taken my seat when the chobdar appeared and asked, 'Who is this Karimuddin Saheb? He has come to Huzoor-e Wala's mind.'

---

* What is now most commonly known as the Red Fort was originally titled Qila Mubarak, the 'auspicious fort'. Baig notes that, in the Delhi of which he writes, the emperor's home was also referred to as the Red Haveli or just Haveli—clearly an ironic diminutive.
† The hall of public audience.

I had only to hear this to break out in a sweat. I had thought that visiting Hakeem Saheb would be enough to resolve the matter. How could I have known that the royal presence itself would require my appearance, and that too before my breath had settled! But the order of the king! What cannot be cured must be endured.

I got up and followed the chobdar, reciting the ayatul kursi* all along our way. I didn't even dare raise my eyes to see where the god-fearing fellow was taking me. I had long nursed a desire to see the Fort from within. Now, with the chance before me, I couldn't gather the courage for even a peek!

We walked so long, I began to feel blind. Finally, thank God, the chobdar left me to stand by the stairs leading up to the Diwan-e Khaas† and went inside to announce my arrival.

Hazrat Jahan Panah was gracing the hamam.

Those who have not seen Delhi's Fort may not understand what it means to sit in the hamam in the summers. The fact is that the hamam is actually a magnificent building with two sections, one hot and the other cold. The part of the building that faces the Moti Masjid is warm, while the one facing the banks of the Jamuna is cold. On this side, a cool chamber has been made by hanging curtains of khas. A stream flows within, and there are several hauz, little tanks, in the middle of the room, from which spring fountains. What hamam—it is actually a piece of heaven!

---

* Verses from the Quran, usually recited to ward off evil or problems.
† Hall of private audience.

Having left, the chobdar showed no sign of returning. Waiting in the sun, I was in torment, drenched in sweat. As I stood with my head bowed, beads of perspiration trickling down my nose, I thought of turning back. However, first of all, it would be highly improper to leave after being summoned; and second, who knew the way? By the grace of God, my suffering was ended when the chobdar returned and said, 'Come!'

This one word, on its own, brought a tremor to my feet and a quiver to my heart. Even so, stepping this way and that upon my own feet, I entered the hallowed hamam. The chobdar called out, 'With respect! Steady your gaze! Hazrat Jahan Panah Salamat. Offer your salutations!'

Thanks to Nawab Zain-ul-Abdeen Khan Saheb, I had come well-prepared for this test. Bowing low, far below waist-level, so much so as to be almost doubled-up, I made seven slow, elaborate salaams, and offered nazr.* While making the salutation, as my eyes rose, I saw the splendour on display.

Hazrat Peer-o Murshid was reclining on a silver cot, with Mirza Fakhru seated at one end, pressing his feet.

Who in Delhi hasn't seen Hazrat Zillulah! Of medium height and very frail, with a rather long face and large, bright eyes below which the bones stood out; a long neck and a high jaw, the nose slim and aquiline—of a rich brown colour; with a shorn head and a thin beard growing sparsely

---

* An offering, either gifts or money, made to rulers and saints, according to the rank and ability of the giver.

on the cheeks and rather more on the chin; and a neatly clipped moustache. He was over seventy years old and his hair had turned snow white, though yet a few black strands stood out in his beard. His face was wrinkled, but no matter his age and weakness, his voice retained a firm tenor. He was dressed in a pair of narrow one-bar pyjamas of green kamkhab cloth and a white kurta of Dhaka muslin. Before him, on a low wooden stool, there lay a robe of jamawar silk and a four-cornered karchobi chogoshya cap.*

Now for Mirza Fakhru. Aged about thirty-two or thirty-three, he was the spitting image of his father. If there was a difference, it was only this: the one was old, the other young; the one's complexion had darkened with age, the other had a more open, wheatish colour; the one had a white beard, the other's was black as ink—otherwise, it might have appeared as if one king was recumbent and the other seated.

Both appraised me intently, and Badshah Salamat said, 'Aman.† Are you the one they call Karimuddin? It seems you hail from some other town?'

I replied, 'Your slave‡ comes from Panipat. From infancy, he has lived under the kind protection of your Majesty, the shadow of God.'

---

* See note on clothing for more details on these fabrics and styles.
† This form of address was common in the Delhi Fort at this time, used for male and female both. Baig notes that it may have derived from an abbreviation of 'Arre' and 'Mian'. It was commonly used in Urdu as a form of informal address until fairly recently.
‡ Literally 'khanazad', that is, 'house-born'.

He said, 'Aman. Mirza Fakhru was talking about you just now. I, too, long to hold a mushaira in the Diwan-e Aam, as once we used to. But what can one do? The times have been struck by an ill wind, and such a thing would be inappropriate now. It is true, as they say, that familiarity breeds contempt—those who share a profession also share rivalries—but God protect us, what is the use of such enmity that it won't allow a moment's conviviality? There would be mushairas in the Diwan-e Aam, and they fared well for a while. But then I noticed a growing unpleasantness and stopped them. Then, Munshi Faiz Parsa began holding mushairas outside Ajmeri Gate, in the madarsa, the school of Ghaziuddin Khan. It fell apart like teeliyan, dry grass. It was a stroke of luck that the radeef was, in fact, teeliyan. God forbid, had it been kariyan—rafters on a roof—God alone knows how many heads would have broken!

'It is all very well that you are organizing a mushaira, but how will you handle the clash of such elephants? Ustad Zauq, poor fellow, is soft-spoken, but God save you from Hafiz Veeran: he is sure to start a fight. You know how a man who cannot see, cannot be controlled: a blind man lashes out blindly. If anyone makes the slightest jibe at Ustad Zauq in the mushaira it will be difficult to handle this heedless gentleman. Mian, I do not see you being able to handle all this.'

I proffered in reply, 'Qibl-e Alam, where would I gather the audacity to consider such a complicated project! It is Nawab Zain-ul-Abdeen Khan Arif Saheb who has taken the responsibility for the arrangements of this mushaira.'

'In that case, I am satisfied. That boy is quick-witted and sharp. He will be able to handle Mirza Nausha and Momin Khan. That leaves Ustad Zauq, and I shall speak to him. If God wills it, then, the mushaira will do well!

'But I tell you this: meet these people before the mushaira. It must not happen that they refuse you at the last moment! I myself and Mirza Shabbo* cannot come; but, of course, I shall send Mirza Fakhru in my place and I shall send a ghazal, too, insha-Allah.

'But tell me, what tarah, rhyme, have you fixed? Rhyme is a cause of great conflict, so think upon it with care.'

The discussion was proceeding thus when a voice rang out from the side, 'Oh, in what an odd position—how be-tarah—has the nurse put the child to sleep!'

On hearing this, Badshah Salamat declared, 'There you are: a faal, an augury, has come to your aid on its own. Don't fix any rhyme scheme at all for the mushaira. Let every man recite his verse in whatever metre and rhyme he desires. *Na lena ek, na dena do.* No challenges to take, nor comparisons to make.'

I asked him, 'Will you declare the date, Peer-o Murshid?'

He said, 'Make it the 14th of Rajab.† It is a good day and it will be a moonlit night. Today is the 5th, which leaves nine days, enough to make all the arrangements. It

---

* Bahadur Shah Zafar's eldest son, Muhammad Dara Bakht, also known as Mirza Shabbo, and heir-apparent at this time.

† Seventh month of the Hijri calendar.

will be the 20th of July and the weather, too, would have cooled down. Now: Khuda hafiz.'

I offered prayers for his long life and prosperity, and backed away from him with light-hearted steps.

Mirza Fakhru said nothing all this while, but I understood that this was all his doing—who was I, otherwise, to merit a private royal audience! How true it is that all odds are evened out with God's blessings.

At this point, however, let me say that the audience was less taxing than leaving it . . . backwards. Unsure of where to place my feet, I had retreated just a few steps when I bumped against a wall.

Still recovering from that collision, I stepped into the stream. Still, with some difficulty, I managed to leave and, no sooner had I come out of the hall than the chobdar joined me. I gave him a tip and got rid of him, and returned to Hakeem Saheb. He was waiting for me. I gave him a full account of what had transpired and he said, 'Maulvi Saheb, the fact is that Mirza Fakhru has long been yearning for a mushaira. This is certainly his doing, or such a matter would hardly have been decided so casually. But come, your work is done. Go and inform Mian Arif; he must be at my house, waiting for you.'

When I reached Hakeem Saheb's house, I found that Nawab Saheb was indeed waiting there for me. I told him how things stood and he said, 'Well, that's one problem solved. Now do this: at the very least, take the trouble to call on Ustad Zauq, Mirza Nausha and Hakeem Momin Khan. But tread very, very carefully. All three are men of great pride. If there's the slightest impropriety in your conversation, bear in mind that the bird in hand will fly away. And if you sense one of them slipping away, mention my name. I trust they will then agree. Second: the haveli of Mubarak-un-nissa Begum, where your press is—empty it out in two days and let me have it. I will need to make our sitting arrangements there.'

'And where shall I go?' I asked.

'Come to my house for eight or nine days. It'll be some inconvenience to you, but what can be done? When we are inviting people from the Fort, we must have the house prepared to match their stature. Let us see what the cost comes to!'

'What can a mushaira cost? At the most, we may spend a hundred or a hundred-and-twenty-five rupees,' I said.

Nawab Saheb smiled at this and said, 'Mian Karimuddin, what would you know of how much is spent on such mushairas? If the whole thing is managed within a thousand or two, consider that you've got away cheap!'

At this, I felt I was losing my senses. I said, 'Nawab Saheb, if this is how things stand, I shall have to offer my salaams to this mushaira from a safe distance. Forget the press, were I to sell myself I wouldn't be able to raise such a sum!'

He said, 'My dear fellow, don't involve yourself in this matter of money. God will solve this problem, too. Now that I have lent a hand to this enterprise, it is for me to work it out and see it through. You sit back and watch the show. But yes, vacate the building by tomorrow. Only nine days are left: little remains of the evening and there's still so much show to put on!

'Now go, Khuda hafiz. You must be tired. Rest a while, and plan how to clear the building by tomorrow morning and make the rounds of the three ustads at home.

'As soon as the building is vacated, let me know and come straight home. Where is the shame in it? After all, it's because of me that you're leaving your own house.'

From there, I went home. By the time I had closed the press and packed all my things, it was evening. On awaking in the morning, I sent my clothes and bedding to Nawab Zain-ul-Abdeen Khan's house, then set off towards Kabuli Gate, to make an auspicious start with Ustad Zauq.*

His house is near Kabuli Gate. It is a very small house. A tiny entrance has a lavatory at one end. Within, the courtyard is so small that when two cots are laid out, there's hardly any place to move about. In front is a small verandah, with a room on top of it. A passage from the courtyard leads to the zenana.

When I reached, I found the ustad sitting on a bare charpoy in the courtyard, smoking a hookah. On the second charpoy was his favourite disciple, Hafiz Ghulam Rasool *Veeran*. He is blind, and it is he whom Hazrat Jahan Panah had warned me to be wary of.

In build and stature, Ustad Zauq is of average size. His complexion is a rather darkish brown and his face heavily

---

* Literally, with the intention of doing the Bismillah—making a beginning with Allah's name—with Ustad Zauq

pockmarked; his eyes big and bright and his gaze piercing. Every feature of his face is distinct and sharp.

That day, he was wearing narrow white pyjamas with a white kurta and an angarkha—also white. On his head was a muslin topi with a round brim.

At the sound of my footsteps, Hafiz Veeran called out with a start, 'Who is that?'

I said, 'Karimuddin. I have come to present myself in the service of Ustad Zauq.'

Hearing his name, Ustad said, 'Come, come. Please come inside.'

I offered my aadaab, and he said, 'Sit down, bhai.'

I sat down next to Hafiz Veeran, on the charpoy.

He said, 'What brings you here?'

I replied respectfully, 'My hope is to arrange a mushaira at Qazi ke Hauz. The date is fixed for 14 Rajab. If it would not be beyond the compassion of your honour to grace the occasion with your presence . . .'

I had only said this much when Hafiz Veeran grew agitated. He began to say, 'Go, go away! From where have you sprung this mushaira? Ustad doesn't have time to waste. Why don't you go to that Mirza Le Paalak* instead of bothering Ustad unnecessarily?'

---

* 'Paalak' means to be brought up, adopted. Baig notes that a rumour was then afloat that Ghalib was the offspring of an unknown Kashmiri and had been adopted by his purported family. Ghalib was, of course, Zauq's greatest rival, which explains Hafiz Veeran's animosity.

Ustad intervened, 'Bhai, Hafiz Veeran, your tongue won't stop wagging! You manage to pick fights with the world without even getting up.'

Hafiz Veeran said, 'Ustad, when he speaks ill of you, why should I sit quiet? For their every insult, they'll hear a hundred from us! Forget the rest, even Mian Ashufta is puffing out his chest. It was only yesterday that he was calling you a naora!* I gave him such a piece of my mind that he'll remember it his entire life. Went through seven generations of his ancestry with a fine comb!'

Laughing, Ustad replied, 'No, dear fellow, no. Why do you get into such squabbles because of me? Let them say what they please. I have replied to them all in this rubayee:

Tu bhalaa hai to buraa ho naheen sakta, Ay Zauq
Hai buraa woh hi ke jo tujh ko buraa jantaa hai
Aur jo tu khud hi buraa hai to woh sach kahtaa hai
Kyon buraa kahne se uske tu buraa mantaa hai

If you are worthy you cannot be wicked, O Zauq,
it is he who's wicked who reviles you;
And if you have faults, then he tells the truth,
why fault him then for speaking ill of you?

---

* Another bit of snide Delhi gossip at the time was that Zauq hailed from a family of barbers, thus 'naora', a barber's son. Baig writes that Muhammad Azad, in writing that Zauq's father was a soldier, had turned his razor into a sword.

I made my own submission. 'I had an audience in the royal court yesterday. Hazrat Zill-e Elahi declared that he would depute Mirza Fath-ul Mulk Bahadur to attend on his behalf, and that he would honour the mushaira with one of his own ghazals. And it was also declared that he would inform Ustad Zauq, who would certainly attend the mushaira.'

These words took the steam out of Hafiz Veeran, and Ustad said, 'Yes, bhai, now I remember. Yesterday evening, Hazrat Peer-o Murshid said as much to me, and it was also commanded, 'You, too, must go.' Mian, insha-Allah, I'll certainly come. But tell me, what tarah has been fixed?'

I told the whole tale, and said, 'Hazrat Zill-e Subhani has done away with the whole dispute over the tarah. Each man may recite his ghazals in whatever metre and rhyme he likes.'

Ustad said, 'Excellent, excellent!', but the frowns on Hafiz Veeran's brow wouldn't go away. He kept muttering, 'May God show kindness, let us see how this mushaira turns out. Hazrat Peer-o Murshid sits around inventing strange ideas.'

He kept talking this way as I got up, offered my salaams and left.

The second target was Asadullah Khan Ghalib. I went via Chandni Chowk to Ballimaran. Right opposite the house of Hakeem Mahmood Khan Saheb runs the lane of Qasim Jaan. The very first house on the left was Mirza Ghalib's. This house is behind a masjid and has two doors, one for men, the other for women. There is also a passage to the women's quarters through the men's section in the house. The porch of its outer gate is somewhat worn and sunk. There is a room above the gate, and at both ends of the room are two tiny chambers. It is in one of these that Mirza Saheb spends the hot summer afternoons. Beyond the gate, there is a smallish courtyard with a series of pillared halls right in front.

When I reached, he was in the inner verandah, reclining on a bolster and writing.

Mirza Nausha [as Ghalib was also called] must be about fifty years of age; a handsome and cheerful-looking man, tall and broad with rather round features. He has a fair, ruddy complexion tinged with yellow—a colour proverbially called champai.* Two of his front teeth are broken. His beard is full, but not dense; and on his shaven head sits a tall, black cap of fur, a bit like a papakh. He was wearing white and narrow one-bar pyjamas, a white muslin angarkha, and over it a pale yellow chogha, a robe, of jamadar silk.

Upon my arrival, he raised his eyes while still writing. I made my aadab. He responded and indicated with his eyes that I should sit.

I had just sat down when Nawab Ziyauddin Ahmad Khan arrived. He is the brother of Aminuddin Khan Saheb, the Nawab of Loharu. He writes Rekhta† poetry as *Rakhshan* and Persian poetry as *Naiyar*. Aged about forty, he has few equals in his essays, geographies, histories, genealogies, biographies of Hadith narrators, lexicographies,

---

* See 'A note on complexion', page lxxvii.
† Urdu or Hindustani.

and his general knowledge. He is Mirza Nausha's disciple and successor.

Short in height and very fair in complexion, with delicate features, heavy-lidded eyes, a sharply cut beard and lean figure—in short, he is a beautiful man. He was dressed in one-bar, narrow white pyjamas and a white angarkha, and on his head was a four-cornered chogoshia topi that had been well shaped on a hat-mould. A large kerchief folded into a samosa-like triangle was draped across his shoulders.

I got up and salaam'd him. He stepped forward, shook my hand with both his, moved aside quietly and sat down on his knees, dozanoo,* most gracefully.

A few moments later, Mirza Ghalib became free of his writing. He turned to Nawab Saheb first and said, 'Mian Naiyar! When did you arrive? Bhai, this Mirza Tufta has made my life miserable. The pest's inspiration never runs out: in every letter he sends me eight or ten ghazals to correct. I get tired advising him.'

Turning to me, he said, 'You are Maulvi Karimuddin Saheb, perhaps?'

'Ji, yes,' I said.

He said, 'Well sir, I have already had news of your visit. Mian Arif arrived only yesterday and extracted a promise from me to attend the mushaira. Well, Mian Naiyar, will you also come?'

---

* To sit on one's knees, with one's weight on the heels of the feet. The posture connotes deference.

Nawab Saheb said, 'Where you go, I follow. If it should please you to attend, insha-Allah, I shall certainly accompany you.'

'But Alai hasn't yet come, bhai?' asked Mirza Saheb, 'I've been waiting for him since yesterday. Oh, there you go, he's arrived! You have a long life, bhai, I was just asking about you!'

Nawab Alauddin Khan *Alai* is the Nawab of Loharu's heir, some twenty-three or twenty-four years old, of wheatish complexion and round-faced, with flat features, light eyes the colour of cool sharbat, and a full beard. He was dressed in narrow pyjamas, with a white jamdani angarkha. Over it, an open, black velvet nima—a half-sleeved jacket; and on his head, a black velvet chogoshia topi. He, too, offered his aadaab, sat to one side and said, 'It's true, I was delayed today. I realized that you must be waiting.'

He looked at me and asked, 'This gentleman?'

Mirza Nausha told him the whole story, and said, 'Alai, you too must come. You are not, I suspect, going to Loharu just yet?'

He said, 'Of course. If you grace it, I shall be present.'

When this matter, too, was settled, I took my leave.

Once free, I returned to Nawab Zain-ul-Abdeen's house. He had cleared a part of the mardana for me. I found all the luggage I'd sent in the early morning, neatly arranged.

I took off the day's clothes. Lunch arrived from within, and I slept a while after eating. Around four o'clock, I woke up and prepared to visit Hakeem Momin Khan.

Hakeem Saheb's house is in Cheelon ka Koocha. On the way, I met Maulvi Imam Baksh *Sahbai*. He was my teacher in college. Of a light wheatish complexion with a few pockmarks on his face and flowing locks on his head, he is a very slight man. He must be about forty years old. He usually wears narrow white pyjamas, a white angarkha and a jubba, a robe, embroidered in the Kashmiri style; and ties a small, white safa—turban—on his head. He lives in Cheelon ka Koocha, too.

'Where are you off to?' he asked me.

I replied, 'To Hakeem Momin Saheb.'

'What work do you have with him?'

I told him, and he said, 'Come, I am going that way, too.'

Khan Saheb's house was right in front of the well-beaten path leading to Hakeem Agha Jaan's house.* It has a large entrance and a spacious courtyard, with buildings all around it. On two sides are two tiny courtyards and, in front, immense halls, one after the other. There is a room on top of the first hall, and the terrace of the hall in front of it has been made the room's balcony, though its parapet is very low.†

---

* Momin's house was in front of the 'chatta'—a well-beaten path—leading into Hakeem Agha Jaan's house. Clearly, this pathway was a kind of landmark of the times; even today, the area is named 'Chatta Agha Jaan'.

† Baig writes that he had seen Momin's house some two decades before writing, reduced to rubble. The low parapet he mentions was to be the cause of Momin's death. He fell off the terrace, was badly injured and died subsequently. Momin had composed the chronogram of his own death: 'with the breaking of hands and feet'.

The floors of the halls are covered with sheets of cotton. At the very centre of the inner hall is spread a carpet, on which sits Hakeem Saheb, reclining against a bolster. In front of him are Hakeem Sukhanand, alias *Raqm*, and Mirza Rahimuddin *Haya*, sitting respectfully, dozanoo. It appears as if a durbar is in progress. No one presumes to look up, or to speak without cause.

Hakeem Momin Khan was about forty years old. Tall, he had a fair and rubicund complexion, on which there shimmered the hint of a five o'clock shadow. His eyes were large and bright, with long eyelashes and brows. He had a long, delicate nose and thin lips, coloured with the lac of paan, and teeth tinged with black missi; a light moustache, a close-cropped beard, stocky shoulders, a slender waist, broad chest and long fingers. The hair on his head was curly and long, the tresses falling on to his back and shoulders, though some had been curled into ringlets by his ears.

On his person, he wore a sharbati-coloured muslin angarkha of the low-cut neechi choli style, but there was no kurta underneath so a glimpse of his skin showed through the fold of the angarkha. Around his neck was a thread of black lace, strung with a golden amulet. A purple dupatta had been folded and wrapped around his waist, with both ends falling in front. In one hand, he held a slender hedgehog. On his legs were red pyjamas of exquisite gulbadan silk, narrow at the ankles but somewhat looser above. Sometimes he would also wear narrow one-bar pyjamas, but no matter what its kind, it was always silken and expensive, with its nefa* wide and red.

The angarkha's sleeves were cut from the front—at times they would hang loose, or else he would roll them up. On his head was a two-piece dopalli topi of gulshan, edged with thin lace, so big that it covered the whole head, and so delicate and translucent that the parting of his hair, his forehead and hair were clearly visible through it. Indeed, he was a well-dressed person, upon whom good clothing sat wonderfully.

When the two of us reached, he was saying to Saheb-e Alam Mirza Rahimuddin Haya, 'Saheb-e-Alam, your chess puzzles are really trying my patience. One or two would be all right, but how long can one meet these daily demands!'

Saheb-e Alam said, 'What can I do, Ustad? These puzzles come to Resident Bahadur† from abroad. Some I solve myself and return to him, but the ones I cannot understand, I bring to you.'

Hakeem Saheb raised his eyes, looked at us and, acknowledging our salaams, he said, 'Sit, please sit.'

We sat down and he returned his attention to Saheb-e Alam. 'Mian Haya, the puzzle you've brought is not, I think,

---

* The nefa is what pyjama strings run through; one may think of it as the loops that hold the 'belt'.

† That is, the British Resident in Delhi, a man far more powerful, at this time, than the Mughal Emperor to whom he would show a token deference. It would be difficult, if not impossible, for anyone in Delhi to refuse the Resident's requests.

too complicated. You say the red will be checkmated and I say, No, the green. Spread the board, and I'll explain.

'And now let me talk to Maulvi Sahbai. And you, Mian Sukhanand, you sit and wait. I have already divined that until this lizard's pair arrives from the east, it shall not move from the wall in front of us. Let its pair come . . . and it *shall* come.'

Sukhanand was a hakeem. He wrote poetry as *Raqm*. He lived in Dharampura and was aged about forty. He was Shah Naseer's disciple in poetry and Khan Saheb's in the art of divination. He was a very well-dressed, well-mannered, courteous, witty, affable, handsome and attractive man. He showed his teacher the deference a son would show his father. As Hakeem Saheb spoke, he said, 'Very fine, most apposite!'

Having conversed with him, Hakeem Saheb turned to us and said, 'Arre bhai Sahbai, it's been many days since you came! Tell me, I hope all is well? And who is this gentlemen with you?'

Maulvi Saheb said, 'He was once my student in college and has now opened a press and wants to organize a mushaira there, for which he has come to trouble you.'

Hakeem Saheb laughed and said, 'Now sir, please excuse me from mushairas. Delhi mushairas are no longer fit for the civilized. There is that one gentleman who raids mushairas with his gang.* Not that any of them has the

---

* Baig explains that this was an allusion to Ustad Zauq, who usually appeared at such occasions with young and aristocratic acolytes from the Fort.

discernment to appreciate a verse, but they will freely raise a din of wah, wahs and subhan Allahs* and spoil the mood. They don't understand that:

> *Saib, do cheez me shikanand qadre sher ra*
> *Tahseen-e naashanaas-o sukoot-e sukan shanaas*

> Saib, two things a verse of worth devastates:
> Discernment's hush and the ignorant's prate

'There is another gentleman who takes Hudhud along with him wherever he goes, and takes on the masters pointlessly. He won't come forward to contest himself but puts his inept hangers-on into the fray. The other day, when that animal recited this verse:

> *Markaz-e khur e gardun be lab-e aab naheen*
> *Nakhun-e qause qazah shibhai mizraab naheen*

> The centre of the sun in the sky is not a surface of water
> The nail like a rainbow is not a fret for playing, no mizrab†

—and said that he had composed it in the style of Ghalib, I cannot describe the disgust I felt. Forget composing like

---

* Bravo, Glory to God—both used as terms of appreciation.
† Such use of complex metaphors was typical of Ghalib. Here the poet has confused complexity with convoluted imagery, either to make fun of Ghalib or flatter him with imitation. A mizrab is a fret.

Ghalib, let him or his Ustad even begin to understand Mirza Nausha's poetry!

'Now, that leaves Mir Saheb. Well, his problem is of another kind. He, too, spouts absurdity, but he doesn't attack anyone. In fact, mushairas become quite lively thanks to him.

'Bhai, it's for all these reasons that I've stopped going to mushairas.'

I tried again. 'Ustad Zauq and Mirza Nausha have already promised to attend the mushaira. Hazrat Zill-e Subhani's ghazal, too, will come.'

He replied, firmly, 'Every man is master of his own will: he may come or send his ghazal. I shall neither come nor shall I send a ghazal.'

We were talking thus when a trader from Banaras arrived with two bundles of cloth. A stop at Hakeem Saheb's was a must for any cloth-trader who came to the city. Hakeem Saheb was in love with silk. If he liked a piece of cloth, then its price was of no consequence. He would pay whatever was asked.

This trader came and took down a bundle from his mazdoor's* head. A lizard fell *plop* from it and ran to climb the wall in front. The lizard that had so long been stuck to the wall scurried to meet it; and having met, the two of them went off together.† We sat there, staring at the play.

---

* Labourer.
† Baig writes that he heard this tale from an eyewitness to it.

When both the lizards were gone, Hakeem Saheb said, 'Well, Mian Raqm, did you see?'

'Ji, yes. I made an error in one part of my calculations; and for insisting on my opinion, I apologize.'

'Bhai, it's only human to make mistakes. And yes, bhai Sahbai, in the matter of the mushaira, my answer is clear.'

When I saw that Khan Saheb was indeed slipping out of my hands, I remembered Nawab Zain-ul-Abdeen Khan's trump card.

I said, 'My connection to this mushaira is only in name. All the doing is really Nawab Zain-ul-Abdeen Khan Arif's. He has grown very ill and lost all hope of living much longer. His last desire is to see a mushaira before he dies, one in which all the masters of Delhi are assembled. He would have appeared before you himself, but Hakeem Ahsanullah Khan Saheb has forbidden him from stepping out.'

This last bit I appended on my own initiative.

Khan Saheb listened to me with grave attention. When I fell silent, he turned to Maulvi Imam Baksh, saying, 'It is a shame, in a man of such intelligent and cheerful disposition, such despondency at such an age! It's true, forever lives the name of Allah!'*

He looked at me and said, 'All right, bhai, you carry on. Tell Arif from me, "Mian, I shall certainly come."'

When I saw how this magic had worked wonders, I sought to expand my reach a little and said, 'Nawab Saheb

---

* That is, only God's name lives forever, mortal matters are more ephemeral. An exclamation of resignation, a way of saying, 'What can be done?'

also said that if you were to bring Maulvi Sahbai, Mufti
Sadruddin Saheb and Nawab Mustafa Khan Saheb *Shefta*
with you, it would be a great kindness.'

Hakeem Saheb said, 'Mian Sahbai I shall speak to just
now. That leaves Azurda and Shefta. So, on your way back,
call on them, too? Tell them that I have sent you. And yes,
what date has been fixed? Where will the mushaira be held,
and what will the tarah be?'

I told him the date and gave him the address of the
house; and I told him all the talk about the tarah that had
happened with Hazrat Jahan Panah.

He said, 'Our Badshah Salamat is a peculiar man.
Whatever comes to his mind is unique. There may never
before have been such a mushaira, in any place, where
no tarah was fixed. Well, at least it's welcome that there
remains no cause for disagreement. On the other hand,
bhai, it is also a fact that without a hint of competition,
one can't really put one's heart into composing verses, nor
derive much pleasure from reciting them.'

Having said this, he grew absorbed in looking through
the cloth, and I offered my salaams and left.

Mufti Sadruddin Saheb's house was near Chitli Qabar in
front of the Azizabadi haveli. Nawab Mustafa Khan Saheb
Shefta lives nearby, in Matia Mahal. On reaching Mufti
Saheb's house, I learnt that Shefta, too, was sitting with him.
Well, I thought, I couldn't have found a better moment. Now
I'll meet them both together. With this thought, I went in.

The house is built in the kothi style, combining both
Indian and English elements. The courtyard is not very big.

It has a little stream. In front are a number of open halls and to the side are English-style rooms. The outer hall has been fixed with a door and thus shaped into a room. Connecting the halls is a high platform, on which takhts* are laid out, covered with cotton sheets and with bolsters on either side. Mufti Saheb and Nawab Saheb are sitting on the takhts, talking.

Mufti Saheb was about fifty-six or fifty-seven years old. A plump figure, nut-brown in colour, with small, sunken eyes, he had a full beard and is a man of very simple ways, not at all given to flaunting himself. He wore white pyjamas of one bar, a white kurta and a small turban, also white.

Nawab Mustafa Khan Shefta, on the other hand, came second only to Hakeem Momin Khan in matters of fashion and dressing. His complexion was dark brown but he had been gifted wonderful features. On such a face, his black, rounded beard looked very good. His build was somewhat heavy and height middling. He would not dress too formally, either. He usually wore white pyjamas, narrow at the ankles, a white kurta, a low-cut white angarkha in the neechi-choli style, and a five-cornered qubba-numa panchgoshia topi. He was about thirty-nine or forty years old.

I offered my aadaab and sat on my knees, dozanoo, on the corner of a takht. Mufti Saheb asked the reason for my visit. I conveyed Hakeem Momin Khan's message and Mufti exclaimed with great amazement, 'Khan Saheb had

---

* A takht or chauki is a low wooden board, variously provided with coverings and cushions.

vowed never to go to a mushaira! Bhai Shefta, what's going on here? One minute it was that he wouldn't go himself, now he's dragging others off with him!'

I related the state of Nawab Zain-ul-Abdeen Khan Arif.

He said, 'Ah, you should have said so. So that is the situation. Otherwise, I was astonished—Hakeem Saheb at a mushaira! All right bhai, tell Arif that Shefta and I will both come.'

Once at liberty, I felt as relieved as a man who's washed off his sins in the Ganga. I returned home in great humour and told the whole story to Nawab Zain-ul-Abdeen Khan Saheb. He, too, was satisfied. When I told him what had happened with Hakeem Momin Khan, his eyes welled up with tears. He said, 'Mian Karimuddin, do you even know that there is a rift between Hakeem Saheb and myself?'

'What are you saying, Nawab Saheb! I cannot describe how troubled he was to hear of your illness. Had it been his own brother, he wouldn't have been so affected. I learnt from Mufti Saheb that he had sworn never to attend another mushaira. It's only for you that he's broken his vow.'

Nawab Saheb said, 'Bhai, what would you know of the affection of these people! They are such people that they cannot even see their enemies in trouble. Anyway, let the matter rest. Now tell me, has your house been vacated or not?'

I replied, 'Ji, yes, it is empty. If you command, I shall be there to assist you.'

He said, 'No, bhai, no. When two men join hands on a project, it is sure to be bungled. You leave the arrangements to me. Let my work be mine to deal with. In fact, do not even come there. If you come and detect any defects, I'll have double the work fall upon me!'

Tarteeb

Arrangements

Ba shero sukhan majlis aaraastand
Nashishtand-o guftand-o barkhaastand

To recite poetry an assembly they arranged,
gathered, conversed and then dispersed

As Karimuddin keeps himself occupied—and out of the way—Nawab Zain-ul-Abdeen Khan makes the most magnificent preparations for the mushaira. On the evening of the gathering, Karimuddin can hardly believe how his humble printing press has been transformed into a glittering garden, decorated with every mark of elegance and refinement. Karimuddin has barely caught his breath when the poets begin to stream in—as sparkling and many-splendoured as the lamps that light the venue. Amongst them are ageing aficionados and ustads, an ascetic genius who walks in naked as the day he was born, and the fashionable troupe from the Fort, dressed to the nines and carrying pet quails. Last to arrive is the Mughal prince, Mirza Fakhru—and, with him, the mushaira may finally begin.

I grew so engrossed in translating *Tareekh-e Abul Fida** that I didn't even step out of the house for seven or eight days. Nawab Zain-ul-Abdeen Khan's passion was such, however, that despite any weakness or fatigue, he set out every morning, and it would be eight or nine at night before he was home again. Therefore, I hardly saw him enough to ask how things were going; and so these eight days passed in a flash and the day of the mushaira dawned.

On the 14th of Rajab, at about half past seven in the evening, I got ready to go to the mushaira. When I asked about Nawab Saheb, I learnt that, having left in the morning, he hadn't yet returned. Stepping out of the house, I found a great commotion in the bazaar. There was talk of the mushaira on every tongue. One would say, 'Who is this Mian Karimuddin?' and another, 'Bhai, whoever he may be, he's made such arrangements as delight the heart.'

Listening to all this and feeling secretly overjoyed, I reached Qazi ke Hauz—and what did I see! On both sides of the road there is scaffolding strung with illuminated glass lamps that turn night into day. The road has been sprinkled generously. Water carriers are offering cool water to passers-by. Mubarak-un-nissa Begum's haveli's large gates have been decorated with lampshades and chandeliers to look like an illuminated garden. From the main gate to the courtyard, there is such light that it dazzles the eye.

---

* The memoirs of Abul Fida (1273-1331), a Kurdish prince and historian. The Karimuddin on whom Baig has based his narrator did indeed translate this work into Urdu.

When I set foot inside the house, I felt almost faint. 'Ya Allah, is this really my house or have I wandered into some royal palace!'

Again and again, I looked this way and that, wide-eyed. 'Wah, Mian Arif, wah! You've really worked wonders! From that poor Karimuddin's lodging to this royal pomp! Really, you were right to say that if the work is done in two thousand rupees, we should consider it cheap!'

The house had been whitewashed with limestone and mica so that the doors and walls sparkled. The courtyard had been laid out with takhts in such a way that it rose to the level of the central platform, the chabutra. The takhts were spread with durrees covered with cloth, with a border of carpets and rows of bolsters. Chandeliers and crystals, lamps of different styles with all kinds of shades, lanterns hanging from the ceiling and fixed upon the walls were arranged in such profusion that the whole house had become a fount of light.*

Whatever the eye saw, it was beautiful and perfectly set. There was a small, green shamiana of karchobi-embroidered velvet at the centre of the first row, set on gold-and-silver Ganga-Jamni† pillars strung with green silken cords. Under the shamiana was a masnad, a seat of honour, covered with green karchobi, on which was a bolster, also embroidered

---

* Baig uses the specific names for lighting gadgets of different types and styles, for example, qandeel, jhar, fanoos, deewar geer, qumquma, handi, hoondi, shamaa, etc.

† Engraved work of mixed metal, usually gold and silver.

with green karchobi.* Eight silver fanoos lamps with green kanwal lampshades were fixed upon the shamiana's four pillars. Strings of crystal-like jasmine were arranged along the length of the poles, the plump buds strung like sehras.† The strings at the centre were gathered together and tied with gold-and-silver kalabatoni threads, with brocade at every knot. They were strung from the four poles in such a way that they created floral doors on every side of the shamiana.

Garlands of flowers hung from doorways, on pegs that already existed, or from nails newly hammered in. White cloth with green borders was stretched above the courtyard, from one end to the other to make a chattgeeri, ceiling. From the very centre of the chattgeeri hung strings of jasmine, the garlands pulled to every side so that an umbrella of flowers was made.

Water was arranged in a small courtyard: empty cups of clay kept ready and surahis‡ coated in saltpetre lined up. Paan was being prepared in another courtyard, and all the paraphernalia for hookahs was carefully arranged in the kitchen. Well-dressed servants stood respectfully at regular

---

* This was evidently the seat made for the mushaira's most distinguished guest, the prince—Fath-ul Mulk Bahadur. A 'masnad' can be anything ranging from a low throne to a cushion or decorated carpet, covered with expensive velvet or silk and richly embroidered. Baig notes that green was the royal colour of Delhi.

† Sehras are worn by bridegrooms in many kinds of Indian weddings, a small curtain of jasmine flowers falling across the face.

‡ A long-necked clay-pot used for storing water and keeping it cool.

intervals. The whole house gave out the sweet aroma of musk and ambergris.

Before the carpets, positioned at regular intervals, stood rows of hookahs, so neat and clean they might have been brought from a shop just then. Between the hookahs there were small stands bearing khasdaans.* In every khasdaan, on a bed of cloth dipped in sweet rose paste, lay paans, already rolled, arranged in such a way that a layer of flowers lay between each. Alongside the khasdaans were small trays of cardamom, milk-soaked betel-nut and bun-dhaniya.†

In front of the masnad were two silver candlesticks with camphor wicks, encased in two small, light green kanwal lampshades. Below the candlesticks were small silver basins filled with fragrant kewra water.

In sum, what can I say? It was an extraordinary spectacle! I was like Abul Hasan‡ from the Arabian Nights—whichever way my eye turned, there my gaze was fixed!

I was still captivated by the spectacle when people began to arrive. The first to come was Karimuddin *Rasa*. He is of royal blood, aged somewhere in his seventies. His erudition is rather low but he considers no one his equal in poetry. He is very kind-hearted, civil and simple natured, with no tinge of duplicity or mischief-mongering. Boatmen

---

* A covered pot meant to hold paan, rolled and ready to eat.
† A mixture of roasted coriander seeds, dried coconut, raisins, dates and other dry fruits.
‡ A character from the Arabian Nights, Abul Hasan was transported in his sleep to the caliph's quarters, where he woke up astounded by his lavish surroundings.

say a man should be first to step into a boat and last to step out. He has adapted this maxim to mushairas. He is the first to arrive at a mushaira and it isn't until every other man has left, one by one, that he will even think of getting up.

It happened, one day, that a mushaira was going on and great clouds gathered overhead. Everyone hurried to finish the mushaira and went home. But he, a stickler for the form to which he was bound, would not get up until everyone else had left. Yes, he would peek out every so often to look at the sky. In such time, it began to rain heavily, pouring down with such force that it flooded everything and everywhere. Some two hours later, when the downpour eased with God's mercy, he, too, got up. But now it was pitch dark, and you couldn't find one hand with the other. The owner of the house gave him a servant with a lamp. The lanes were knee-deep in water and this poor man's feet in expensive zardozi shoes. How to slosh through the mud! At last, he muttered to the servant, 'Give me your shoes.'

But what were his shoes—just contraptions to put one's feet into! Still, he dragged himself along in them, with his own shoes tucked under his arm. On reaching the Fort, he gave the servant a new pair of shoes, saying, 'You have done me such a kindness as I shall not forget my entire life. Whenever you need anything, come to me.'

Over time, the rogue troubled him greatly. To begin with, he went around town proclaiming his secret; and besides, he'd arrive every other day to cadge a few rupees off him. But Mirza Saheb never refused him and would do him a favour whenever the man went to him.

Nawab Zain-ul-Abdeen Khan Saheb stepped forward to receive him at the carpeted end of the floor, and asked, 'Hain, Saheb-e Alam, Mian Haya didn't come with you?'

Mirza Rahimuddin Haya is his eldest son, but father and son have been estranged for a while now. Nawab Saheb had only to say this that Saheb-e Alam exploded like an angry boil, 'Nawab Saheb, why in the world would he come with me? Ever since he's returned from Banaras, he's been a different person. Of what standing is a poor creature like me—he pays no attention to anyone now! Nurtured and cared for him, brought him up, gave him an education, made him a poet, taught him to fight quails—I swear by the throne*—taught him such tricks of quail-fighting that let alone in the Fort, not even the most accomplished in the art across Hindustan would know! And now, the same young prince, forget acknowledging me his teacher, feels ashamed to even call me Father! Haan bhai, why not! It is the thirteenth century!† And by sending him to Banaras I invited disaster: first my own loss, then the smirks and snickers of others. My son slipped out of hand and brought constant bickering, day and night.'

He was speaking thus as Nawab Saheb led Mian Rasa to a seat and had him settle down.

Nawab Saheb was just free from him when a group of princes arrived, with Hafiz Abdur Rahman *Ehsan* in

---

* Baig writes that it had become customary in the last days of Mughal rule for princes to swear by the throne or the crown, political conditions being so uncertain that every potential heir thought he might be the next king.
† By the Hijri calendar, of course.

their midst. Who in Delhi doesn't know 'Hafiz Jio'! He is a universal ustad. Once, the whole Fort followed him but, as soon as Ustad Zauq stepped into the Fort, his sway began to wane.

He, too, has seen the changing colours of time. He has faced Shah Naseer.* Even in his old age, he stepped up to face challenges and, until his last breath, never retreated from a contest. He is about ninety years old, doubled from the waist like a bow. He was the Balaam Baora† of his times, but would recite ghazals in such a booming voice as would overwhelm a mushaira.

He had long been acknowledged an ustad. First he became the ustad of Mirza Neeli. Gradually, his reach extended to Shah Alam Padshah Ghazi, Noor-ullah Marqadha‡, Allah Illuminate his Grave, who used to call him Hafiz Jio, which is how he became famous through the Fort by that name.

He was masterly at completing a couplet, and could quote authorities with such alacrity that any critic would be left open-mouthed.

One day Badshah Salamat recited,

Subh bhi bosaa tu detaa mujhe aye mah naheen

Even in the morning, O Moon, you won't give me a kiss

---

* Shah Naseer was an ustad of the previous generation, who taught Zauq and Momin among others. He died in 1838.
† The prophet Balaam, a diviner in the Torah.
‡ Shah Alam II, grandfather of Bahadur Shah Zafar.

Pat came the response,

Naamonasib hai mian, waqt-e sehargaah naheen

It isn't proper mian, no more is it the morning's bliss.

Someone objected to the formation of '*Waqt-e sehargah*' and he promptly quoted Saeb:[*]

Aadmi peer chun shud, hirs-e jawaan migardad
Khwab dar waqt-e sehargaah giraan migardad

When a man grows old, his jealousy grows young,
sleeping in the morning becomes troublesome.

—and the critic stood gawping red-faced.

A very lean man with a very dark complexion, he was caricatured for his colour by Shah Naseer in this verse:

Aye khaal-e rukh-e yaar tujhe theek banata
Per chod diya hafiz-e Quran samajh kar

O mole on the face of my love, I would have set you right
But let you go because you were hafiz[†] of the Quran.

---

[*] Saeb Tabrizi (1592–1676), a great Persian poet, considered a master of the ghazal.
[†] Hafiz: someone who knows the Quran by heart.

Nawab Saheb received each of them with great warmth and sat them at their places.

He was still busy seating them when Munshi Mohammad Ali *Tishna,* stark naked, swayed and staggered in, in drunken ecstasy. He is a young man of eccentric temperament. Often, he will lie about entirely nude; sometimes he puts on clothes and becomes a fairly normal person. He is no one's disciple and he is everyone's disciple. Sometimes he goes to Hakeem Agha Jaan *Aish* for advice and sometimes he takes his ghazals to Ustad Zauq for corrections.

He has been given an unusually sharp mind. Lakhs of verses sit on the tip of his tongue. He needs only to hear a couplet to have it memorized. It has often happened that having heard and memorized someone else's ghazal, he recites it as his own at a mushaira, leaving the other poor fellow gaping.

Nawab Saheb came forward and asked, 'Munshi ji, what is this style?'

He said, 'The authentic style. When does the mushaira begin?'

Nawab Saheb said, 'It will start any minute, but do sit first.'

So he went off to a corner and sat down. Mian Arif brought a doshala shawl and draped it upon him. He threw it off and remained seated, unperturbed, in the very naked state in which he had arrived.

Now, people began to stream in. Nawab Saheb would receive everyone who came and escort them to their place.

Hakeem Momin Khan came, and with him Azurda, Shefta, Sahbai and Maulvi Mamluk-ul Ala. Maulvi Saheb

is the headmaster in Madarsa-e Delhi. He is a marvel of a
man. The madarsa has benefitted from his blessed self in a
way that would be rare at any time, for any teacher. He
is entirely bound by the Shariah and will not, therefore,
recite poetry himself. His discernment is such, however,
that when he praises a verse, it means that the verse will last.

He is about sixty and belongs to Naanoota but has
been coming to Delhi for a long time. Night and day,
he's absorbed in study and scholarship and rarely goes to
mushairas. Perhaps Maulana Sahbai dragged him here.

It was only recently that the poor fellow's devoutness and
asceticism put him in a real fix. It so happened that Resident
Bahadur came to inspect the madarsa and, in consideration
of Maulvi Saheb's learning and rank, shook hands with him.
As long as Saheb Bahadur remained, Maulvi Saheb kept
the hand away from himself, as an impure thing is kept far
away, and washed his hand meticulously and many times
as soon as Saheb left. Someone carried the tale to Saheb.
It made him very angry—to have honoured the man with
a handshake only to be insulted in return! The matter was
buried with great difficulty.

Maulvi Saheb was my teacher, too, so I came forward
and offered my aadaab. He said, 'Mian Karimuddin, I
had never hoped for so much from you! You've left even
the Delhiites behind. Subhan Allah, subhan Allah, what
arrangements! I'm delighted to see them! May God give
you the spirit to do even more.'

I said, 'Maulvi Saheb, what am I, and what is my ability!
All this is the doing of Nawab Zain-ul-Abdeen Khan.'

'Bhai, this is a fine thing!' he said. 'The one says that the entire arrangement is Karimuddin Khan's, and you say it's all Nawab Saheb's! Come, I'll hail you a Haji and you can do the same for me!'*

All this was going on when Mirza Nausha alighted from his palanquin. Naiyar, Alai, Salik and Hazeen were with him. Mirza Ghalib headed straight to Momin Khan, shook both hands with him and said, 'Bhai, Hakeem Saheb, a letter came today from Mohammad Nasir Jaan *Mahzoon* in Azimabad. He has sent you many greetings and regards. I don't know why he left for Patna so suddenly. A grandson of Khwaja Mir Dard†—I, at least, did not like his leaving Delhi. Now he pines for friends, and just see what sorrowful lines he's composed:

Na to naama hi na paighaam zubani aayaa
Aah Mahzoon, mujhe yaraan-e watan bhool gaye

Neither letter nor word ever reached me
Aah Mahzoon, my friends from home have forgotten me

'Arre bhai, the night is dark already and Mian Ibrahim [Zauq] hasn't yet come—when will this mushaira finally begin?'

Momin Khan was about to reply when a voice called 'Assalam-o Alaikum!' from near the door.

---

* A Persian proverb, meaning two persons joined in mutual praise or profit; similar to 'I scratch your back, you scratch mine.'
† Khwaja Mir Dard (1720–1785) was among Delhi's greatest poets.

Maulvi Saheb [Sahbai] said, 'There you go, Mirza Saheb, Ustad's advance guard has arrived, Hafiz Veeran Saheb—and your friend Hudhud is with him too. Let us see whom he pecks at today.'*

Mian Hudhud's name is Abdur Rahman. He hails from the east. After coming to Delhi, he's been living with Hakeem Agha Jaan *Ayesh* and teaches his children. It was at Hakeem Saheb's suggestion that he took the pen name *Hudhud*; and with his encouragement that he grew a thin beard on his chin, shaved his head and tied a small turban on it, and thus began to look like a good and proper hoopoe.† It was through Hakeem Saheb that he made his way to court and was titled 'Tair-ul erakeen, Shahpar-ul mulk, Hudhud-ul shoara, Minqar jung bahadur—Bird's Pillar, Renowned in the Realm, Hoopoe of Poets, Valiant Beak in Battle!'

In the beginning, his humorous verses would enliven a mushaira, but later he began attacking the ustads. It is said that he did so at Hakeem Agha Jaan's instigation but, whatever it may be, people began to develop a kind of contempt for him, and instead of making fun of others he became the butt of jokes himself. Hakeem Saheb could not take his side openly, nor did Hudhud have what it takes to parry the witty jibes of Delhiites, so he would soon grow limp and surrender the argument.

---

* Literally, 'Ustad's elephant signal has arrived', that is, Zauq is preceded by his faithful Hafiz Veeran as a king might be preceded by a troop of elephants.

† Hudhud means hoopoe, sometimes mistakenly identified as a woodpecker.

Hudhud was forever needling Mirza Nausha and Hakeem Momin Khan, which is why Mirza Nausha smiled at Maulana Sahbai's use of the phrase 'your friend' and said, 'Bhai, why would I entangle myself with him? But let us see . . . there is a Moses for every pharaoh* as they say. I hear that our Mir Saheb is to hold forth in honour of Maulvi Hudhud this evening? If this stalwart versifier is able to withstand him, I shall accept he's accomplished a great deal.'

They were talking thus when Ustad Zauq arrived. The whole Fort had come out with him and, having exchanged greetings, they took their places and sat down.

Those of the Fort and those connected to them have a peculiar manner of doing the salaam. Standing straight, they lift their right hand to the ear, as one does for the namaaz, then let it drop. There, the salaam is done. Others salaam in the usual way.

Fort people are so distinctive, they may be recognized at a glance. Whether princes or nobles of royal lineage, they all look alike in appearance and dress: the same long neck, the same slim, high nose, long bookish face, large almond eyes, large mouth and front teeth, the cheekbones standing out below the eyes and a deep, nut-brown complexion, the beard thin on the cheek and dense on the chin—in sum, the kind of similarity there is among these people would be rare in any family. From Amir Temur's time to this day, there has been no change in their features.

---

* A Persian proverb implying that every tyrant has his nemesis.

Earlier, the Fort had only one way to dress, but now the styles have become more varied. The reason is that ever since Sulaiman Shikoh* attained influence in the court of Awadh, some in the family have settled there, while others keep travelling to Benares. Whosoever comes from there brings new cuts and drapes, which results in something of a mishmash style, half-partridge–half-quail, neither of Lucknow nor of Delhi.

Now just look at the people sitting right here. Those princes who have returned from Lucknow have the smaller Lucknowi dopalli topis on their heads, angarkhas with high-cut oonchi cholis over fine sharbati muslin kurtas and narrow pyjamas. Those who never left the Fort are wearing the same old dress: chogoshia topi, angarkha with low-cut neechi choli under a velvet or jamawar kaftan and one-bar pyjamas of striped gulbadan or ghalta silk. Those who have come from Lucknow, you may call Delhi princes if you will, but their dress and style make them typical of Lucknow alone.

Ustad Zauq met everyone and sat to the right of the central shamiana. Seating poets at a mushaira by proper order is an art. I must compliment Nawab Zain-ul-Abdeen on how he manged to make everyone sit where he wanted them to, and that too in such a way that no one complained or took offence.

---

* Sulaiman Shikoh was a Mughal prince of the late eighteenth and early nineteenth centuries. He spent some years in exile in Awadh, with its grand capital in Lucknow, and patronized a number of poets.

If someone went and took a seat that Nawab Saheb deemed inappropriate then, instead of making him move, he would go and sit at a more suitable spot himself. After a moment, he would say, 'Arre bhai, can I have a word?'

The guest would come and sit with him and Nawab Saheb would speak to him for a while, in which time a gentleman whom he considered suitable for the vacated seat would arrive and he would say to him, 'Please sit, there's an empty place!'

Once that spot was filled, he would get up, having thus arranged two seats in one stroke.

Seating the princes is a bit more tricky. They take offence at the slightest thing and walk out with 'Wah! I? And sit here!' Then you may coax them all you will, they won't listen.

Ustad Zauq understood these tussles very well and so arranged for his companions himself, with such dexterity that none of them even imagined they were being 'arranged' for the occasion. He would say to one, 'Saheb-e Alam, please come here'; and to another, pointing at a chosen spot, 'Sit, bhai, sit!'—and thus, shortly, the whole gathering was settled.

It was arranged thus: to the right of the meer-e moshaira* was the group from the Fort, and to his left were the other ustads of town and their disciples.

---

* The chief guest; in this case, Mirza Fath-ul Mulk Bahadur, also known as Mirza Fakhru.

One thing that struck me as strange was that all the Fort-walaas were holding on to quails. This fever for quail- and cock-fighting has spread across the Fort. Every day there are bouts between partridges, quails and cocks.

There was one prince who created a real spectacle. On a large cart, he built a small 'house', covered its roof with mud and planted it with millets. In this 'house'—God save me from speaking a lie!—there were lakhs of tomtits! He would take the cart wherever he wanted and fly his birds. The birds are so well trained that not one ever leaves the hut. Let him only wave his flag and they fly, and let him but sound his call and they return to perch on the roof.

It was only a few minutes after Ustad Zauq's arrival that Mirza Fath-ul Mulk arrived in his open palanquin, his havadar. With him was Nawab Mirza Khan *Dagh*.[*]

Mian Dagh is sixteen or seventeen years old. His complexion is quite dark, but with a wonderful tenderness in the features, large eyes with drooping lids, an aquiline nose, an ample forehead, on his head a black velvet-laced chogoshia topi, on his frame an angarkha of colourful saslet, gulbadan pyjamas and a silk handkerchief in his hand. He is still young, of course, but the poetry he composes—Subhan Allah! His ghazals are sung across the city.

The havadar was lowered to the ground. Mian Dagh stepped out and stood to one side. Then, Mirza Fath-ul

---

[*] Dagh's mother had married Mirza Fath-ul Mulk after Dagh's father, Nawab Shamsuddin's execution (see Introduction). This, writes Baig, explains Dagh's arrival with the prince.

Mulk alighted; his feet had only to touch the ground for everyone else to spring to their feet.

Four chobdars wearing tall green khirkidar turbans and long green achkans, jackets, with silver-lace banat embroidery, red shali kerchiefs tied to their waists and carrying either Ganga-Jamni maces or peacock-feather whisks, morchals, had followed the havadar. As Mirza Fakhru stepped out, the mace-bearers arranged themselves before him and the morchal-bearers behind. This small procession proceeded with slow deliberation towards the shamiana. Mirza Fakhru stopped near the shamiana and accepted everyone's salaams. Then he looked all around and said, 'With your leave?'

'Bismillah, bismillah',* everyone replied.

He walked into the shamiana, greeted everyone and sat down. Everyone else stood awaiting his permission to sit. He looked around and said, 'Please take your seats!'

Everyone salaam'd and sat down. Ustad Zauq gestured to Dagh to come and sit near him, and he went and sat there. The morchal-bearers stood behind the shamiana and the mace-bearers positioned themselves behind the front row.

Once all this was done, Nawab Zain-ul-Abdeen Khan came forward, offered his tasleemaat† near the shamiana and

---

* Literally, 'I begin in the name of Allah'; implying please go ahead in the auspicious name of Allah.

† A very formal manner of greeting or obeisance usually reserved for royalty, which involved bowing low from the waist while raising the right hand to

sat down dozanoo. He spoke softly to Saheb-e Alam for a moment, then returned to his place.

Once he had returned, Nawab Fath-ul Mulk raised his hands for the fateha and all the gathered raised their hands with him.*

Following the prayer, Saheb-e Alam addressed the gathering, 'O you sweet-tongued versifiers of the garden of Delhi, what cause have I, with masters like yourselves before me, to harbour any thought of presiding over this mushaira! It is only in deference to Hazrat Peer-o Murshid's command that I have brought myself here—otherwise, who am I to aspire to the honour of leading such a grand mushaira!

'Dear friends, you know the special feature of this mushaira, that no tarah has been set for it. A second feature you may discern is that not one but two lamps shall circle the gathering.† Just as the door of arrogance and prejudice has been closed by removing the tarah, so, with two lamps in circulation, any anxieties about the order of reciting, such as often darken the disposition, will disappear. The desire to begin or end a mushiara, too, often creates schisms.

---

the forehead—thus symbolically offering one's head to one's superior. The gesture is made three or seven times.

* The fateha is the first chapter of the Quran, and a prayer offered for welfare. Baig adds that Mirza Fath-ul Mulk was known to be very pious and would begin no work without prayer. Thus, he was called 'mulla' or 'mulatia' in the Fort. (A popular pun on his name is Fateha-ul-mulk).

† The form of reciting at a mushaira was that a lamp would be placed before the poet who was to recite, and the order of recital would ascend from the junior-most poets to those of highest ability or rank. In the normal course of things, therefore, Emperor Bahadur Shah Zafar's ghazal would have ended the mushaira.

For this mushaira, I have made the end the beginning. This mushaira will begin with the inspired composition of Hazrat Zill-e Subhani, after which, by submitting my own ghazal, I shall remove any distinction between the beginning and the end.'

Having said this, Mirza Fakhru made a sign. Two chobdaars were standing in front. Each picked up a lamp and brought them before him. With a Bismillaah, he removed their lampshades, faanoos, and, having lit the lamps, put the fanoos back. The chobdars took the lamps, placed them on shallow trays, paraats, stood upright and looked towards Mirza Fakhru. Mirza Fakhru nodded. At the sign, both called out, high and loud, 'Gentlemen, the mushaira begins!'

The cry rang out and a long hush fell. The Fort-wallas stuffed their quails into bags and put them behind their bolsters. Servants hurried to clear away hookahs, replacing them with spittoons, khasdans and saucers of bun-dhunia, and returned to their places.

In this time, the palace khawaas* arrived from the Fort with Badshah Salamat's ghazal. Several heralds accompanied him. He came to the lamps, bowed in tasleemaat and asked for leave to recite the ghazal. Mirza Fakhru indicated his permission with a nod. The khawaas sat down where he was and the heralds called out, 'Gentlemen, the miraculously inspired verses of Hazrat Zill-e Subhani Saheb Qiraan-e Sani Khuldullah Mumlika-o Saltanata are to be recited. With utmost respect, listen from the depths of your hearts!'

---

* The royal eunuch or main attendant.

Takmeel

Accomplishment

Huzoor-e shah mein ahl e sukhan ki azmaish hai
Chaman mein kush nawaayan e chaman ki aazmaish hai

An audition of able poets before the king
As in a garden, a trial of sweet singing

Finally, as evening falls, the mushaira begins with a verse by Emperor Bahadur Shah Zafar himself. Two lamps are circulated amongst the assembled poets, and as the lamp arrives before each one, he recites the ghazal he has prepared for the occasion. Each poet has his own eccentricities, and they exhibit varying levels of talent and competitiveness—all remarked upon in amusing asides by Karimuddin. There are moments of both farce and ecstasy, culminating, as dawn begins to rise, in recitals by the three great masters—Momin, Ghalib and Zauq. The morning azaan fills the air, and the poets disperse.

At the heralds' call, the gathering sat up dozanoo, and everyone bowed their heads respectfully. The khawaas took out the king's ghazal from its case, kissed it, touched it to his eyes and began to recite at a lofty volume in the note of sorath.* The choice of words, the beauty of the language, the flow of meaning and, most of all, the reciter's voice cast a spell. A hush spread from the earth to the sky. Everyone was too enthralled to even utter a word of acclaim. The masters swayed at every couplet. Occasionally, a whispered 'Subhan Allah!' might escape someone's lips but, otherwise, the mehfil was in a trance.

At the maqta, it was as if everyone had been spellbound. Every man swayed in rapture. Following unanimous demand, the maqta was read out several times, and the sweetness of the words was delighted in.

Here, you read it too, and enjoy the language:

Naheen ishq mein is ka to ranj hamein
Ke qaraar-o shakeb zara na raha
Gham-e ishq to apna rafeeq raha koi aur
Bala se raha na raha
Na thee haal ki jab hamein apne khabar
Rahe dekhte auron ke aib-o hunar

---

* Sorath is a type of raga most popularly associated with hymns from the Sikh scripture, the Guru Granth Saheb. Like all ragas, the sorath creates a particular feeling and atmosphere. The writer and musician Vasudev Murthi attempts to capture its effect in these words: 'Your mind will dive deeper and deeper into the depths of your soul, finding more and more and yet returning effortlessly to the present, understanding that the restlessness of the outer world is an illusion that has to be endured till your soul is ready to move on from its temporary home.' (Vasudev Murthi, *What the Raags Told Me.*)

Padi apni buraiyon par jo nazar
Toh nigah mein koi bura na raha
Hamein saghar-o bada ke dene mein ab
Kare der jo saqi to hai ghazab
Ke yeh ahd-e nishat ye daur-e tarab
Na rahega jahan mein sada na raha
Lage yun to hazaron hi teer-e sitam
Ke tarapte rahe pare khak pa hum
Wale nazo karishma ki teghe dodam
Lagi aisi ke tasma laga na raha.
Zafar aadmi us ko na jaaniyega,
Ho wo kaisa hi sahib-e fahmo zaka
Jise aiyesh mein yaad-e khuda na rahe
Jise taish mein khof-e khuda na raha

Not of *ishq* do I make this complaint
that peace and patience I was left without;
The agony of *ishq* kept me company, no matter
whatever remained—or did not.
When on my own self I had never thought
I sat judging others' shame and their honour.
My gaze, when it fell on my own many blots,
then in my eyes others' faults were wiped out.
If now in serving my goblet of wine
Saqi delays, it will be a crime
that this joyous, hedonistic time
will never exist, as it never has.
So many the arrows of torment have struck
that long I lay tossing in pain in the dust

But the two-edged sword of flirtation and lust
struck me—the strings of my armour were cut.
Zafar, do you not know him a man
who, howsoever sagacious and grand,
when he is at ease, remembers not God,
and when in a rage, who fears his God not.

Having read the ghazal, the khawaas gave the script to
Mirza Fakhru. The ghazal was written on gold-dusted
paper, in Hazrat Zillullah's own hand—the penmanship so
immaculate that it mesmerized the eyes. Mirza Fakhru took
the paper and looked around.

Mamluk-ul Ala put a hand on his heart and said, 'Saheb-e
Alam, where do we have the words to praise Hazrat Zill-e
Subhani as we should? Still, we express our gratitude for the
royal favour that Hazrat Peer-o Murshid has bestowed on
this mushaira by sending us his ghazal. May we be honoured
by having our most insignificant gratitude proffered in the
king's court.'

Mirza Fakhru turned to the khawaas. He said, 'Qibla-e
Alam, I shall take this message to the Peshgah-e Aali as soon
as I reach.'

The khawaas was about to pay obeisance and leave
when Mirza Fakhru stopped him. 'Before you leave, you
might as well recite Saheb-e Alam-o Alammian Hazrat
Waliahad Bahadur's ghazal.* He honoured me with it just

---

* Muhammad Dara Bakht, or Mirza Shabbo, was Mirza Fakhru's older half-
brother. As the current heir to the throne, he was too exalted, like the
emperor himself, to attend the mushaira.

as I was leaving and asked me to have it recited by a sweet-voiced man—and where shall I find one more melodious than you?'

With these words, he took the ghazal out of his pocket and handed it over to the khawaas, who took it with an aadaab, and recited the ghazal from where he sat.

Dil se lutf-o mehrbaani aur hai
Mehrbaani ki nishani aur hai
Qissa-e Farhad-o Majnu aur hai
Ishq ki mere kahaani aur hai
Rokne se kab mere rukte hain ashq
Balke hoti khoon feshani aur hai
Hum se aye Dara woh kab hote hain saaf
Un ke dil mien badgumaani aur hai

A heart's fond embrace is one thing,
Grace manifest, quite another.
Tales of Majnu and Farhad are one thing,[*]
what my love entailed, quite another.
As if my tears would ever stop at my bidding—
instead there flows blood, more freely than ever.
Is he ever, O Dara, in my favour fair?
His heart's hesitation is of another order.

The ghazal was quite insipid, but it was Waliahad Bahadur's after all. Who had the nerve to not praise it! Even so, Ghalib

---

[*] Majnun and Farhad are romantic heroes in Arabic and Persian literature.

and Momin sat absolutely quiet. Some Fort-wallas felt bad about it, but they knew these two perfectly well—that they were of the kind who only offered genuine admiration. The Waliahad was all very well; should Badshah Salamat's own ghazal be weak, they wouldn't favour it with so much as a nod!

Be that as it may—the khawaas read the ghazal and went on his way, and it came the turn of the gathering to recite. Mirza Fakhru motioned to the chobdar, who brought both the lamps and placed them in front of the shamiana. Mirza Fakhru took out his ghazal, looked around, bowed his head a fraction, and said, 'I hardly dare recite in competition with masters of the craft such as yourselves, but whatever I have, good or bad, I submit in the hope of being corrected.'

> *Gham woh kya hai jo jaanguza na hua*
> *Dard woh kya jo la-dava na hua*
> *Haal khul jayein ghair ke sare*
> *Par karoon kya ke tu mera na hua*
> *Dard kya, jis mein kuch na ho taaseer*
> *Baat kya jis mien kuch mazaa na hua*
> *Woh to milta, par aye dil-e kamzarf*
> *Tujh ko milne ka hausla na hua*
> *Shikwa-e yaar aur zubaazn-e raqeeb*
> *Khel tahra, koi gila na hua*
> *Tum raho aur majma-e aghyaar*
> *Mera kya hai, hua hua na hua*
> *Phir tumhare sitam uthane ko*
> *Ramz achcha hua, bura na hua*

What is grief that wounds not the soul!

Is it pain when it may be cured!

My *ghair's* affairs may fall open, apart,

but you won't be mine—then what do I do!

What is anguish that leaves not a mark!

What is talk without wit, on the whole!

He would have met me, but O feeble heart,

to face him you were not so bold.

Complaint of my *yaar* from my *raqeeb's* tongue

is merely for play, not real reproach.

You in a throng of my rival stalwarts,

what of me, if I'm there—or if I am not!

To endure once again all of your scorn

that Ramz grew better—may not be so bad.[*]

Mirza Fakhru's voice was not particularly strong, but his recital held such pathos that it would wrench the heart. The whole mushaira resounded with cries of 'Wah, wah!' and 'Subhan Allah!'

At the third couplet Mirza Ghalib, and at the fifth Hakeem Momin Khan called out 'Wah, wah!' with such fervour that they slid ahead of all the others by their side. Mirza Fakhru continued reading his ghazal, but these two were stuck on those two couplets and kept repeating them, reciting and swaying in ecstasy. When the ghazal ended, Mirza Nausha said, 'Subhan Allah, Saheb-e Alam, subhan Allah!

---

[*] Ramz was Mirza Fakhru's pen name.

Wah, what can I say! This is how a sher is composed. What great pleasure!'

Ustad Zauq, too, smiled, thinking, 'Well, in this guise, I am praised, too.'[*]

Mirza Fakhru got up and salaam'd, 'It is your affection, as elders, that makes you encourage me, though I know of what little account I am.'

Wherever he looked, people would praise him, and he would bow and salaam. When some calm had returned to the mehfil, Mirza Fakhru gestured to the chobdar. He picked up a lamp and placed it before Mian *Yal*, in the opposite row.

His name was Abdul Qadir, but every child in town knew him as Mian Yal. He was so proud of his own strength that he had no regard for any other wrestler. Whichever akhara he went to, he would go and throw an open challenge that no one would have the courage to accept.[†]

---

[*] Zauq, as the emperor's ustad, would also have tutored all the princes in the Fort, including Mirza Fakhru.

[†] An akhara is a school for wrestling and other martial arts; popular public institutions across much of northern India, where youngsters are trained by ustads. Baig includes a long and lovely footnote to his tale at this point, telling of how Mian Yal's pride led to his fall:

Finally, it was this pride that proved to be his downfall. People didn't like his daily boastful challenges in the akhara. Haji Ali Jaan, ustad of the Shekhuwalon akhara, coached a youngster. Not too pronounced in build but well-versed in strategy, and what to say of his speed!

One day, when Mian Yal walked into the Shekhuwalon akhara and began throwing his weight around, as usual, the boy took off his clothes, leapt in front of Yal, beat his thighs and held out his hand [thus offering a wrestler's challenge].

It was from wrestling that he had derived the pen name
of Yal. His poetry was a bit rakish. He recited like someone

Mian Yal burst out laughing—how could this upstart match him! He hesitated to shake hands.

Ustad Ali Jaan said, 'Why bhai, won't you shake hands? Either accept the fight, or never bring your challenges to this akhara again.'

'Ustad, just look at the match,' said he, 'why crush this little fellow for no reason?'

Ustad replied, 'Mian, as one sows, so one reaps. Clobber him in the arena. All that will happen is this, isn't it, he'll break a few bones and learn his lesson.'

Finally, hands were shaken and a date was fixed: only a few days after this mushaira, the match was held in the royal arena. It was near the eidgah, prayer ground, and could seat ten to fifteen thousand. That day, you couldn't have fitted a straw in it: only heads to be seen every which way you looked. All of Delhi was on the boy's side because of Mian Yal's vain behaviour.

It began with a few minor bouts. On the dot of four, both men entered the arena wearing loincloths, threw off their chador coverings, chanting 'Ya Ali!'. They rolled over a few times, recited something, rubbed mud on their chests and came face to face, slapping their thighs. There was a world of a difference in their physiques—a match between an elephant and an ant!

The arena was quiet, you hear a pin drop. The only sounds were either 'Ya Ali!' or the slapping of thighs. Mian Yal took the boy's hand and pulled. He bent forward. Mian Yal got on his waist. In a flash, he dived down and escaped. Mian Yal took his right hand and tried to trap him in a *dhobipat* grip. He smashed through and stood aside. Mian Yal would ram him with all his might, but with his speed he would soon break away.

Finally, Mian Yal caught him. The boy crouched quietly. Pinning him down hard, Mian Yal locked him in a grip around his neck and arm, and kept the pressure high. The boy endured it. Mian Yal wanted to open the boy's chest for attack; the boy was awaiting his chance. Mian Yal was a little careless in pulling him up and the boy caught his legs and flung him in such a way that Mian Yal fell flat on the ground, face up. The lad leapt astride his chest. The arena shook with a thousand cries, 'Woh mara, woh mara!'—You did it!

People ran and picked the lad up in their arms. No one even looked to see where Mian Yal was. He got up quietly, wrapped himself in his chador, covered his face, and vanished in such a way that no one ever saw him again. That exit from the arena was his exit from Delhi. He was a self-respecting man: no one saw his face from that day to this.

God knows where he lived and died.

proclaiming war on a battlefield. It mattered little to him if he was praised or not. His only thought was to recite his poem.

The ghazal he'd written was:

Kah do raqeeb se ke woh baaz aye jung se
Hargiz naheen hain yaar bhi kum us dabang se
Lab ka badha diya hai mazaa khatt-e-sabz ne
Saqi ne pusht di may-e safi ko bung se
Dil ab ke be-tarah se phansaa zulf-e yaar mein
Nikle ye kyon-ke dekhye qaid-e farang se
Aa-jaiyo na pech mien zaalim ke dekhna
Yaari to tum ne ki hai Yal us shokh-o shung se

Tell my *raqeeb*—'Back down from the battle!'
For surely my friends are a match for the scoundrel.
A thin wisp of hair adds charm to his lips,
Saqi's spiked wine with *bung* in its barrel.[*]
My heart's badly caught in my lover's tresses,
from such *farang* fetters, let's see how it unravels.[†]
See you're not trapped in the *zaalim's* designs,
though Yal, you've befriended a charming rascal.

His ghazal ended, and the chobdar picked up the second lamp and put it before Mirza Ali Beg. A very fair-complexioned man, fond of exercise too. He used *Nazneen* as his pen

---

[*] *Bung* (like *bhang*) means cannabis.
[†] *Farang* is 'foreign'.

name, and was the only rekhti-go[*] in Delhi. As the lamp was put down, Nawab Zain-ul-Abdeen Khan called out, 'Bring an orhni!'[†]

Immediately, a servant appeared with a deep red orhni, dotted with stars. Nazneen put it around himself with great style, half-covering his head with one end of the cloth, spreading the rest before him—and so he became quite a presentable woman!

He recited the ghazal with such flirtatious gestures and honeyed tones that the whole mushaira began to applaud. He would recite with such sweet mannerisms that even a dancing girl would have been left far behind. The second verse was recited as if by one prepared to go to any length to inflame an elder sister's jealousy.

The Fort-wallas enjoyed the ghazal immensely, but the masters of rekhta sat and listened quietly.

The ghazal was:

> *Hui ushshaaq mein mashhoor Yusuf sa jawaan takaa*
> *Bua, hum aurton mein tha bada deeda Zulaikha kaa*
> *Mujhe kahti hain baji tune taakaa chote dewar ko*
> *Nahee darne ki main bhi, haan naheen taakaa to ab taakaa*
> *Agar aye Nazneen tu dubli patli kaamni si hai*
> *Chareera sa badan naam-e-Khuda hai tere doolhaa kaa*

---

[*] One who recites in the rekhti style. Rekhti began in Lucknow, possibly invented by Saadat Yaar Khan Rangin (1757–1835); it involves a male poet assuming a female persona and style. Rekhti became quite popular but the masters tended to frown upon it.

[†] A woman's veil or wrap.

She gained glory amidst lovers, eyeing Yusuf in his prime;
amongst us girls, O sisters, had Zuleikha gladdest eyes.
Says my baji* 'You made eyes at the young brother of
my groom!'
I'll be not scared, if not yet, I will *now* be so inclined!
If, O Nazneen, you're the slim, lithe and so-loving kind,
Well done, your *doolah's* form in Khuda's name is refined! †

Now the two lamps began circulating in such a way that
first a person to [Mirza Fakhru's] right would read and then
a person to his left. The illustration on page 153 will make
clear the course of the lamps and the arrangement of the
mushaira.

After Nazneen, the lamp moving rightwards came to
Mian *Ashiq*. This poor fellow is a labourer and cannot read
nor write. He isn't anyone's disciple nor anyone's ustad, but
composes well enough. One of his couplets at the mushaira
was such that—Subhan Allah!

It went like this:

Faqat tu hi na meraa aye but-e khoonkhaar dushman hai
Tere kooche mein apnaa har dar-o deewaar dushman hai

Fierce beauty made *but*, you are not my only foe:
your bylane's every wall and every door is my foe.

---

* Elder sister.
† 'Doolah' is bridegroom. Invoking 'naam-e-khuda', God's name, is an
Urdu idiom signifying slightness and tenderness, needing God's protection.

The other couplets in the ghazal were just padding, but the 'Wah, wahs' for these lines went on a long while.

When his ghazal ended, the left-moving lamp was placed before Abdullah Khan *Aouj*. He is a skilled poet of about forty or forty-five and has been around for a long while. Always in search of new subjects, he goes and finds such elevated themes and subtle ideas that let alone expressing them in a couplet, it would be difficult to accommodate them in a qata.* Yet he tries to squeeze several such ideas into one couplet, with the result that his meaning is an utter muddle. How can anyone enjoy or applaud his verses? Well, he recites himself, enjoys himself, and then, all alone, admires himself.

He recites his ghazals with such passion that he bounces yards ahead in his frenzy. He has only a handful of disciples, but even the masters declare him an ustad. After all, who has the inclination to invite an unwanted argument by not calling him an ustad! No sooner has he read his verse than Ustad Zauq or Mirza Ghalib has cheered. Only a slight delay in praise and his face falls, and who dares face his wrath! Willy-nilly, the applause will come; only then will he cool down.

The ghazal:

---

* A qata is a series of couplets that follow the same idea (unlike the usual form of a ghazal, in which every couplet expresses its own idea). Karimuddin suggests, not without a hint of ridicule, that even if Aouj had chosen to elaborate on his themes in a qata, they would have remained difficult to express, let alone understand.

Dum ka jo damdamaa yeh bandhe khayaal apna
Be pul saraat utren hai yeh kamaal apna
Tifli hi se hai mujh ko wahshatsara se nafrat
Sum mein gada hua hai ahu ke naal apna
Kasb-e shahadat apna hai yaad kis ko qatil
Sanche mein tegh ke sar lete hain dhaal apna
Chechak ke ablon ki main baag modta hoon
(Rakh ke) devi ke aastaan par seemeen halaal apna

Such storms of sighs weave through these thoughts of mine,
to cross bridge-less* to purgatory's an expertise of mine.
From infancy have I disdained a wild and frenzied life,
stuck vice-like in a deer's hoof is this birth-cord of mine.
Who remembers now, assassin, my hunt for martyrdom?
I cast it in the mould of swords . . . this head of mine.
I do reverse the tide of the small-pox's pustules,
(offering) to devi's shrine this silver crescent of mine.

Mirza Ghalib sprang upon the last couplet. He said, 'Wah
Mian *Aouj*, you've done wonders with the second line of
this verse. Bhai, how well you brought 'offering' into it!†
They are kafirs‡ who call you 'ustad'. Mian, you are a god
of poetry, a god!'

---

* Literally, 'be pul Saraat', that is, without the bridge called Saraat. Saraat is a
razor-thin bridge that leads to heaven: the good can walk across it without
trouble, but the bad are cut in two by it and fall into hell.

† 'Rakh ke', 'by offering', is not strictly necessary to the meaning of the last
couplet; Mian Aouj uses it purely for the sake of the metre.

‡ One who denies the truth.

All the ustads bundled praise upon him, and Mian Aouj is such that he positively ballooned with glee. When the excitement had subsided somewhat, the lamp slid rightwards to Mohammad Yusuf *Tamkeen*.

He would be about fifteen or sixteen years old, a student at the Madarsa-e Delhi. He has been blessed with a wonderful sense of humour, and speaks so gently and well it is as if flowers drop from his lips. With delicate features, a dark complexion and well-proportioned limbs, he will emerge a very beautiful man in his prime.

His ghazal:

Dauzakh bhi jis se mangta hardam panah thaa
Kis dil jale ki bare khudaya yeh Aah thi
Khana kharaab ho tera aye ishq-e be-haya
Ayeen kaun sa thaa yeh, kya rasm-o raah thi
Tune jo dil ko mere sanam-khana kar diya
Rahtaa khuda tha jis mein yeh woh bargaah thi
Tamkeen ko ek nigaah mein deewanaa kar diya
Jadoo fareb aah ye kis ki nigaah thi

From which even Hell ever sought safe-keeping,
O Khuda, the sigh of which heart's breaking?
O shameless *ishq*, may your house fall to ruin,
what law was this, what manner of loving?
This heart of mine, you made *sanam's* dwelling,
was once that court where Khuda had being.
With a glance who left Tamkeen thus churning,
Alas! whose glance was it, spellbinding?

Everyone praised Mian Tamkeen to give him heart; he was asked to recite his qata many times. Ustad Ehsan said, 'What to say, Mian Yusuf! I'm very satisfied. You compose very well, indeed. Keep at it and you'll be a master one day. But Mian . . . become someone's disciple. Without an ustad, you may fall adrift.'

Mian Tamkeen smiled and said, 'Ustad, can I ever stray from your command? Insha-Allah, I shall present myself in service of Ustad Aouj tomorrow!'

Ustad Zauq said, 'Yes, bhai, yes, a wonderful choice! You will have sailed through in no time, believe me.'

All this talk was going on when the second lamp arrived before Ghulam Ahmad *Tasweer*. He is also called Mian Babban. He can't tell 'A' from 'B' but has a fantastic, natural aptitude. He was once a disciple of Mian *Tanweer's*, then he broke away from him and joined Ustad Zauq.

He has a solid build, clean-shaven with a small moustache and a dark complexion. He wore narrow-bottomed pyjamas of coarse, striped silk and a kurta of the same kind, with a long kerchief on one shoulder and a round cap of simple soozni embroidery on his head.[*]

The poor man earns his living as a hookah tube binder. A poet of great facility, he cannot read or write, so stuffs every word that he composes into his mind and heart. His memory is such that he begins to play like a musical organ

---

[*] Mian Babban was more simply dressed than his fellow poets. Soozni is a simple and functional form of embroidery, nothing like the high fashion preferred by, say, Momin Khan.

at the slightest prompting, and won't think of stopping. His verses are so pure that even the greatest masters are forced to nod. Listening to him, you would never guess that an unlettered man was reciting. Imagine him as an excellent example of the saying 'alshoara talameez ur Rahman', that is—poets are pupils of the Lord.

The ghazal:

Hijr ki shab to sehar ho ya-rab
Woh na aayaa toh qayamat hi sahi
Jaan bekaar to apni na gayee
Aye sitamgar teri shohrat hi sahi
Mujh se etna bhi na khichye saheb
Aap par meri tabiyat hi sahi
Jazba-e dil naheen laya tum ko
Aap ki khair enayet hi sahi

Let dawn break Lord upon this night of *hijr*—
if he won't come, let doom at least engulf me!
My life was not needlessly forfeit, it seems,
if it brought you, *sitamgar*, some glory, at least.
Do not pull away from me so, O Saheb,
even if my yearning is endless it seems.
No, passion does not bring you to me,
still, it will do if it is but to humour me.

The mehfil echoed with an uproar of 'Wah, wah' and 'Subhan Allah' at every couplet. When the ghazal was done, Ustad Zauq looked at Hakeem Momin Khan and said, 'Khan Saheb, this Mian Babban has been endowed with a wonderful talent. He is called my disciple for the sake of form, but I have never yet felt the need to improve any of his verses. Yesterday, he recited a ghazal and I was transported! One couplet was so inspired, it's impossible to praise it enough. Well, Mian Babban, what was the verse?'

Mian Babban pressed upon his memory a little and the lines slipped from his mind to his tongue. Its matla was:

Barchi teri nigah ki pahloo mein aa lagi
Pahloo se dil mein dil se kaleje mein ja lagi

The spear of your gaze through my ribs it struck,
from ribs to heart, from heart to liver it struck.

And this was the verse:

Daaman pa woh rakhe na rakhe dilroba lagi
Lekin hamari khak thekane se aa lagi

He may keep it on his *daaman* or not, it seems to please him—
But I, the dust, have found my home upon him.

Hakeem Saheb praised him heartily, and said, 'Mian Babban, this is God's gift. Such talent doesn't come from book-learning. Bless you, Mian, you've delighted my heart.'

After this, the lamp came to Mohammad Jafar *Tabish*. He hails from Allahabad but came to live in Delhi a long while ago. The poor man is very housebound but in love with poetry. There is no mushaira that he doesn't make his way to.

Two verses from his ghazal are very good. I'll quote only those:

Kabhi bin baada rah naheen sakte
Taoba kuch hum ko sazgaar naheen
Dil mein khush hai odoo par aye Tabish
Woh sitamgar kisi kaa yaar naheen

I am never at ease without my wine,
such penance doesn't agree with me.
Odoo may be glad in their hearts, O Tabish,
but the tyrant's no friend to anybody.

The maqta's composition was so pleasing that 'Wah, wah's' fell from everyone's lips. Mufti Sadruddin's condition was such that he would recite it and sway.

The lamp opposite Tabish came to Mian *Qalq*. May God save you from him! He is a cunning man named Abdul Ala. He is from Madras, about twenty years old. He left home as a child; came to Delhi via Hyderabad. He's ruined thousands, ensnaring them in webs of amulets and charms. People grow fearful at the very sight of him. He proclaims himself Shah Saheb,* but God knows the truth of his heart.

---

* How a Muslim holy man, a saint-like figure or a religious mendicant might be addressed.

His verses are not bad. He had written:

Khumm e sharab se khum e gardoon to ban gaya
Saqi bana de mah peyala uchaal ke
Hum mashribon mein chal ke Qalq maikashee karo
Jhagre wohan naheen hain haram-o halal ke

This pitcher of wine curves like the horizon,
toss up a cup *saqi*, and make us a moon.
Go drink your fill midst your own, O Qalq,
what's proper or not, there no one disputes.

When he finished, the lamp came before Munshi Mahmood Jaan *Aouj*. His ghazal had only two couplets that drew a smattering of praise; the rest of them were mere verbiage.

Aane mein us jaan-e jaan ke der hai
Kuch muqaddar kaa hamare pher hai
Hai yaqeen woh jaan-e jaan aata naheen
Maut ke aane mein phir kyon der hai

The love of my life is late,
which is partly a twist of my fate,
When I'm sure my *jaan-e jaan** isn't coming,
why then is my death so delayed?

Then came Mirza Kamil Beg's turn. He is a soldier by profession, uses *Kamil* as his pen name. Even to the mushaira,

---

* Literally the 'life of life', another term used for the beloved.

he came in his soldier's uniform, reciting his ghazal as if commanding an army. If you look, you'll find a martial tint in his verse, too.

The qata is most enjoyable. I'll quote that alone:

Mizgaan se gar bache hai, abru kare hai tukre
Yeh baat kah ke maine jab usse daad chahi
Kahne lagaa ke tarkash jis waqt hove khali
Talwaar gar na kheeche to kya kare sipaahi

Having escaped the lashes, I am cut by the brow—
jesting thus, when I made my appeal,
he said, 'When the quiver of arrows empties,
has the soldier a choice but to draw out his steel?'

Now it was Hakeem Syed Mohammad *Taashshuq*'s turn to recite. He is a scholar of great repute. Aged sixty-three or sixty-four; no one excels him at hikmat. In truth, what can I say? He is a well-cultivated person but hankers for more than he's worth. When he hears a good verse he grows restless, desiring that 'As I applaud now, so others should praise me!' His verses aren't bad, but nothing to illuminate a mushaira, drawing spontaneous 'Wah, wahs' from every man.

Sample his work for yourself:

Tujh ko is meri aah o zaari per
Rahm aye fitnagar naheen aata
Wada-e shaam to kiya lekin

Kuch woh aata nazar naheen aata
Tere bimar ka yeh aalam hai
Hosh do-do pahar naheen aata

Upon my longing sighs you
take no pity, O *fitnagar.**
He promised me the evening, but
there's little sign that he will come.
Your ailing suitor's state is such,
he lies unconscious for hours.

There was some praise but it didn't quite satisfy his heart,
and he became somewhat despondent.

Next, the lamp came to Mir Husain *Tajalli.* He is Mir
Taqi Mir's grandson, a very humorous and discerning person.
A hint of Mir Saheb's style sparkles in his compositions.
He stakes his all on his use of language; the ghazal may be
quite short but whatever he writes, he writes well. And why
not—whose grandson is he, after all!

Meri wafa pe tujhe roz shak thaa aye zaalim
Yeh sar yeh tegh hai, le ab toh aitbar aayaa
Yeh shauq dekh pas-e marg bhi Tajalli ne
Kafan mein khol deen aankhen suna jo yaar aayaa

Day in, day out you doubted me, *zaalim*
Here's my head and a sword, are you now satisfied?

---

* A mischief-maker, another term for the beloved.

Tajalli's desire behold, look how after he died,
at word of his love, how he opened his eyes!

The second couplet drew such acclaim that Mian Tajalli
was all smiles.

When Mian Tajalli had read, there came the turn of
Hakeem Sukhanand *Raqm*. I had met him in Hakeem
Momin Khan Saheb's house. His composition was not
particularly good but he recites wonderfully. At the
slightest praise from any quarter, he would execute a string
of salaams.

The ghazal he'd composed was:

Bujhana aatish-e dil ka bhi kuch haqeeqat hai
Zara sa kaam tujhe chasm-e tar naheen aata
Adam se koocha-e qatil ki raah mulhiq hai
Gaya udhar jo guzar pher idhar naheen aata
Ho khak chara gari is mareez kee tere
Nazar mein tujh sa koi charagar naheen aata

To douse a heart's flame should not be so hard—
yet this little thing you wet eyes cannot do!
The road to the *qatil* leads to the hereafter
who crosses across cannot return too.
No cure could heal this patient of yours
No healer in sight could ever equal you.

The third couplet was in the style of Hakeem Momin Khan
Saheb, who praised it lavishly but said alongside, 'Mian

Raqm, either practise hikmat alone, or just write poetry.
To do both at once and manage is a bit difficult.'

No sooner did the lamp come to Sheikh Neyaz Ahmad
Josh than all Zauq's disciples sat up. Ustad Zauq holds *Josh*
in high esteem. He is about eighteen or nineteen years old
but unusually intelligent and incisive. His versification and
understanding of poetry is renowned throughout the Fort.
Even so, I didn't like the ghazal he read at the mushaira,
though the Fort-wallas created a great ruckus with their
'Wah, wahs'. Ustad Zauq also encouraged his disciple,
saying 'Subhan Allah, subhan Allah!'

Take a look at the ghazal. It may be that I misjudged it:

Keyonkar woh hath aaye ke yan zor-o zar naheen
Le de ke ek aah so us mien asar naheen
Qismat se dard bhi to hua woh hamein naseeb
Jis dard ka ke chaaraa naheen chaaraa gar naheen
Qismat mein hi naheen hai shahaadat wagarna yaan
Woh zakhm kaun sa hai ke jo kaargar naheen
Sajde mein kyun pada hai are uth sharaab pi
Aye Josh maikada hai khuda ka yeh ghar naheen

Why should he come to me, I lack power, prosperity;
I offer up a sigh, which too lacks potency.
By fortune my fate has brought me such agony,
such agony as lacks healer and cure equally.
Were it not that my fate holds no martyrdom for me,
what wound have I not that would not finish me?
Why are you prostrate, get up and drink deep—
you're in a house of wine, *Josh*, not of divinity.

Did you read the ghazal? I would still say it has no particularly praiseworthy couplet but, of course, to praise from obligation is another matter altogether.

Then came Maulvi Imam Baksh *Sahbai's* elder son, Mohammad Abdul *Aziz's* turn. He uses *Aziz* as his pen name, and composes very fine ghazals. And why shouldn't it be so! He's the son of a great father.

Hai, what couplets he's composed!

Joon shama shaghl tere sarapa neyaaz ka
Jalna jo soz ka hai to rona gudaaz ka
Kaj fahmiyon se khalq ki dekha ke kya hua
Mansoor ko hareef na hona tha raaz ka
Hum asiyon ka bare gunah se jhuka hai sar
Aur khalq ko guman hai hum per namaaz ka
Maghroor tha hi aur bhi maghroor hogaya
Is mein gila naheen mujhe aiyeena saaz ka
Auron ke sath lutf se tha soorat-e neyaaz
Yan barh gaya dimagh taghaaful se naaz ka

Your supplicant's calling is that of a candle—
Burning in passion, with misery melting.
See what happened from common misunderstanding:
Mansoor should never have rivalled the Secret.*
The weight of our sin bows the heads of us sinners

---

* Mansoor al-Hallaj (c. 858–922) was a Persian mystic best known for declaring 'Ana'l haqq', 'I am the truth', a statement that could (and was) interpreted as a claim to divinity. Though Mansoor was a popular Sufi saint and teacher, he was also controversial and eventually executed.

and people believe that namaaz we are reading!
Proud he was and still more so became,
for this the mirror's Maker I don't blame.
Kindness to others brought kindness in him,
neglecting me archly made him the more vain.

Tell the truth—the whole ghazal is exquisite, isn't it? Yes, whatever praise this ghazal received was its due. Ustad Zauq, too, said, 'Bhai Sahbai, this son of yours has turned out wonderfully. May God give him a long life, he will earn great fame. Wah, Mian Sahebzade,* wah—what can I say? I'm delighted. And why shouldn't it be so, the apple doesn't fall far from the tree!'

Mian Aziz got up and salaam'd, and took his seat.

After Mian Aziz, the lamp came to Khwaja Moinuddin *Yekta*. What to say of him? He has been titled 'Khan' by the government and shows no regard for anyone. He is now one man's disciple and now another's. Earlier, he was taught by Ehsan, now he's veered to Mirza Ghalib. Such fickle temperaments have never learnt anything yet, nor ever will. I was glad that nobody praised him. He must have been very upset but who could praise couplets like these?

Aye aah-e shola za, ye khas-o khaar bhi naheen
Nao asman hain do bhi naheen chaar bhi naheen
Hai kis ko taab-e shikwa-e dushman ke zof se

---

* Literally, 'son of a saheb'; a playful and affectionate way of addressing young gentlemen, particularly by their elders.

Lab per hamare tazkirae yaar bhi naheen
Jeena firaq-e yaar mein wade ki lag per
Aasan gar naheen hai to dushwar bhi naheen

O sigh in flames, this is neither husk nor straw,
nine are there skies, two or four are there not.
Unable to decry my rivals in my weakness,
even words of my love on my lips there are naught.
To survive this *firaaq** on only a promise—
if it isn't easy, so hard it is not!

The one to whom the flame came next, now he's a real poet. Who? Mirza Haji Beg *Shohrat*. Fair-complexioned, of medium height, thirty or thirty-two years of age. He lives in great style. Mushairas would be held in his house, once upon a time, though the practice ended a little while ago. He is a virtuous disciple of Mufti Sadruddin. He composes well and recites well too, with a resonant voice, reading in such a way that every word touches the heart.

Each of his couplets was praised and why not—every couplet was worthy.

The ghazal:

Ek din do din kahaan tak tu bhi kuch insaaf kar
Yeh toh jalna roz ka aye soz-e hijran ho gaya
Hai taraqqee johar-e qabil hi ke shayan ke main
Khak se putla bana putle se insaan hogaya

---

* A synonym for hijr, separation.

Kufr-o deen mein tha na kuch oqda bajuz band-e naqab
Uske khulte hi yeh kaar-e mushkil aasaan ho gaya
Pahle dawa-e khudayee us but-e kafir ko tha
Kuch durusti per jo aaj aaya to insaan ho gaya

A day, two days, till when? Be you, too, fair:
it is a daily fire, O this burning separation!
It's progress worthy of the virtuous that I,
a doll made of dust, a doll became human.
A knotted veil alone obscured faith and denial,
the question resolved as soon as it opened.
Once that *but-e kafir* to godhead had claims,
now somewhat reformed, he became human.

Mirza Ghalib was in such a state—enchanted by the last couplet. He would strike his thighs and say, 'Wah Mian Shohrat, wah—you've worked a wonder! This is not a couplet, it's a miracle. This one couplet could stand its ground against the life's works of many poets. Indeed, what a thing you've said, subhan Allah! *Pahle dawa-e khudayee us but-e kafir ko tha / Kuch durusti per jo aaj aaya to insan ho gaya.*'

Indeed, the couplet had cast a strange spell over the gathering. People would recite it to themselves and to each other to better enjoy it, and in their enjoyment they swayed and in their excitement called out, 'Wah, wah!' and 'Subhan Allah!'

It was quite a while before the gathering calmed down and the lamp arrived before Nawazish Husain Khan *Tanweer*.

He is a young man, some thirty-two or thirty-three years old. Badshah Salamat holds him dear, but Mian Shohrat's verses had created such a sensation that no one paid any attention to his ghazal. Besides, the ghazal was quite ordinary. Only this qata was worth noting:

Jaan kar dil mein mujhe apna mariz-e tap-e gham
Kahta logon se bazahir but-e aiyaar hai kya
Range rukh zard hai, tar chashm hai, lab per dam-e sard
Poochna is se ke is shakhs ko azaar hai kya

Knowing me, in his heart, lovesick for him,
what does he tell people, this *but*, scheming?
'His face is pale, eyes streaming, breath cold—
go ask this man what ailment grieves him.'

When he finished, the lamp was placed before Mir Bahadur Ali *Hazeen*. He is a very grave and dignified man, set in his ways. He is a disciple of Arif's. One of his couplets is most enjoyable:

Suboo se munh lagaen-ge ab etna sabr hai kis ko
Ke bhar le khum se mae sheeshe mein aur sheeshe se saaghar
mein

We'll put our mouths to the pitcher, for who has the patience
for wine to drip from barrel to bottle, from bottle to glass!

This is the ghazal he read at the mushaira that day. Two or three of its couplets were good. Everyone liked the maqta, and it is good indeed.

Duniya ki wusatein tere goshe mein aa gayeen
Allah re wusatein teri aye tangna-e dil
Jal jal ke akharash tapish-e gham ke hath se
Ek daagh rah gaya mere pahloo mein jae dil
Dekha woh apni aankh se jo kuch suna na tha
Aur dekhiye Hazeen abhi kya kya dekhaye dil

The whole of the world you did fit in your nook—
Allah re, what a swathe, O you little heart!
Burnt over at last by the heat of my sorrow,
a scar left bereft where there once beat a heart.
I saw with my eyes all I had never heard of,
Hazeen, let us see what it shows now, this heart.

Next, the lamp came to a man who is a poet himself, whose father is a poet, whose brother is a poet, whose entire family comprises poets—and who is he? Mian Baqar Ali Jafri—that pride of poets, Nizamuddin *Mamnoon*'s younger brother; and that king of poets, Qamruddin *Minnat's* younger son. If *his* ghazal lacked spirit, whose ghazal would have any?

Listen to these two couplets. He writes:

Tegh yun dil mein khayal-e nigah-e yaar na kheech
Nakhuda tars! Tu kaabe mein toh talwaar na kheech

Be-saropa chaman-o dasht mein alam ke na phir
Naz-e har gul na utha minnat-e har khar na kheech

Do not, recalling your love's gaze, draw a blade on your
heart;
Have fear, captain! In the Kaaba, at least, a sword do not
draw out.
Rudderless don't wander the world's gardens and wilds,
each rose's whims do not bear, each thorn's pleas do not
draw out.

The ghazal wasn't praised as it should have been. The reason
is that this style seems to be disappearing from Delhi. People
enjoy what is current; whatever's fashioned that way is a hit.
Mirza Ghalib was very fond of this style once, but even he
is giving it up now.

After this, it was Munshi Mohammad Ali *Tishna*'s turn
to read. The chobdar hesitated a little in putting the lamp
before him. Naked as the day he was born, he was seated
dozanoo, swaying joyfully. The chobdar glanced at Mian
Fakhru, who indicated with his eyes, 'Put it down.' The
chobdar set the lamp down. When its light fell on Mian
Tishna's face, he opened his eyes. Imagining it to be God
knows what, he blew out the flame, and said, 'May I offer
something, too?'

'Certainly, please recite', everyone replied.

In his own unique style, half-singing, half-reading, he
presented this ghazal:

Ankh padti hai kaheen paon kaheen padte hain
Sab ki hai tum ko khabar apni khabar kuch bhi naheen
Shama hai gul bhi hai bul-bul bhi hai pervana hai
Raat ki raat yeh sub kuch hai sehar kuch bhi naheen
Hashr ki dhoom hai sab kahte hain yun hai yun hai
Fitna hai ek teri thokar ka magar kuch bhi naheen
Neesti ki hai mujhe kucha-e hasti mein talaash
Sair karta hun udhar ki ke jidhar kuch bhi naheen
Ek aansoo bhi asar jab na kare aye Tishna
Faida rone se aye deeda-e tar kuch bhi naheen

Your eyes fall one way, your feet fall another,
of others you know much, of yourself nothing at all.
There's a rose, a candle, a nightingale, a moth—
all night there is all this, at dawn nothing at all.
In an uproar of doom they say, *It is thus, it is thus*—
just the mischief of Your touch . . . it is nothing at all.
To not be while in the world of being I seek,
I stroll off to where there is nothing at all.
When even a tear falls for nothing, O Tishna,
what gain wet eyes from crying?—nothing at all.

How can I describe the effect of this ghazal? There was utter stillness, enveloping earth and sky. The ghazal's subject, the midnight air, the reader's condition—the mehfil seemed stunned by it all. While it was thus on the one hand, Mian Tishna rose up on the other, waving his arms and repeating 'Nothing at all, nothing at all', and walked out of the door in his euphoria. His 'Nothing at all, nothing at all' rang in our ears a long while.

When people had gathered themselves somewhat, everyone blurted out, 'It is true, nothing at all!'

Mirza Fakhru called for the lamp, had it lit, and said, 'Well, gentlemen, let us continue.'

The lamp was put before Hafiz Mohammad Husain *Bismil*. What impression could he have made after Tishna! For one, he is a novice—he takes lessons from Mirza Qadir Bakhsh *Saabir*—and, for another, there was nothing very impressive about his ghazal. Nonetheless, the maqta was good.

The ghazal:

> *Dil tu ne hum se O but-e kaafir utha liya*
> *Is naazuki pe bojh yeh kyon kar utha liya*
> *Bar-e giran-e ishq falak se na uth saka*
> *Kya jaane mere dil ne yeh kyon kar utha liya*
> *Peer-e mughan ne Bismil mai kash ko dekh kar*
> *Sheesha baghal mein haath mein sagar utha liya*

> Oh *but-e kafir* you took my heart away,
> how will you, so delicate, carry its weight?
> The sky itself cannot hold the weight of love,
> it is a wonder my poor heart carried its weight.
> The old man of the tavern saw Bismil the drinker there,
> put wine-bottle under his arm and picked up the goblet.

Be that as it may, some listened, some didn't. Some faint praise was offered and the lamp reached Mir Husain

Taskeen. He would be about forty or forty-two years old. He is a disciple of Sahbai's, and has taken advice from Momin too. His family is very well-known in Delhi. It was his grandfather, Mir Haider, who killed Mir Hasan Ali, the prime minister of Farrukhsiyar.* A soldierly man, he is not bad at poetry either. He had written:

> *Hazar tarh se karni padi tasalli-e dil*
> *Kisi ke jaane se go khud mujhe qaraar naheen*
> *Shab-e visal mein sun-na pada fasana-e ghair*
> *Samajhte kaash na apna woh raazdaar mujhe*
> *Woh apne waade pe mahshar mein jalwa farman hain*
> *Naheen hai zof se anboh mein guzar mujhe*
> *Mere qusoor se deedar mein hui takheer*
> *Na dekhna tha tamasha-e rozgaar mujhe*
> *Maze ye dekhiye aghaaz-e ishq mein Taskeen*
> *Ke soojhta naheen apna ma-aal-e kaar mujhe*

A thousand consolations for my heart had I to find
at someone's going, though myself I had no peace.
All night of *visal* I had to hear of my *ghair*—
I wish he would not give me such secrets to keep.
He is resplendent, as promised, on judgement day;

---

* Syed Husain Ali Khan Barha was one of two brothers—known to history as the Syed Brothers—who became virtual kingmakers in the Mughal court after the death of Aurangzeb. Farrukhsiyar (r. 1713–19) was emperor only in name, and eventually murdered by the Syed Brothers. The brothers, too, met violent ends when a Mughal prince called Roshan Akhtar (later Muhammad Shah 'Rangila') made his bid for the throne. It was Husain Ali's brother, however, who was the prime minister.

Too weak am I to take my plight into the melee.
I am to blame, I delayed casting eyes upon Him,
too long did I gaze upon life's revelry.
Look at the joys of new love, O *Taskeen*—
that I cannot imagine the end I shall reap!

This ghazal brought some life back to the mushaira and
people sat up attentively. The lamp came to Ustad Ehsan's
student, Khwaja Ghulam Husain *Bedil*. He recited this
ghazal:

Nigah ki, chashm ki, zulfe dotaa ki
Sahe ek dil jafa kis kis balaa ki
Kab us gul* ki gali tak ja sake hai
Hava bandi hai yaaron ne havaa ki
Buton se milte ho raaton ko Bedil
Tumhen bhi din lage qudrat khuda ki

The glance, the eyes, the curled locks—
one heart to bear so many shocks!
Can even a breeze reach the lane of my love!
My friends weave tales of wind with talk.[†]
You do meet beauties at night O Bedil—
you too have your day! Glory to God.[‡]

---

[*] 'Rose', another term for the beloved.
[†] A lovely idiomatic phrase, 'hava-bandana', literally 'to tie the wind', means
to boast or exaggerate.
[‡] 'Din lage' is an idiom that translates as somewhere between being successful
and growing too big for one's boots.

From beginning to end the ghazal was dull. Who would have praised it? But yes, the ghazal that Mohammad Husain *Taeb* recited afterwards, that was very gratifying. Taeb is Maulana Shah Abdul Aziz Mohaddis Dehlvi's nephew, and Fakhrush Shoara Nizamuddin Mamnoo's disciple. He writes delightful ghazals in the short metre, and recites so well that one can't begin to praise him.

The ghazal:

Phir kitan war jigar chak hua
Phir koi Mah laqaa yaad aaya
Kahiye us but ko mushaabah kis se
Dekh kar jis ko khuda yaad aaya
Ahde peeri mein jawaani ki umang
Aah kis waqt mein kya yaad aaya

Afresh my heart rent apart as cloth,
afresh I recall a moon-like face.
Say, whom shall I liken that *but* to,
that vision who recalls God's grace?
In great old age the fervour of youth—
Oh how of a sudden does one reminisce!

The second and third couplets were so greatly appreciated that the audience exhausted itself praising them, and Mian Taeb offering salaams in response.

When the commotion died down, the lamp came to Ustad Zauq's ustad, Ghulam Rasool *Shauq*. The poor man is old now, a disciple of Shah Naseer's, and imam* in the Azizabadi mosque. There was a time, at the beginning of his career, when Ustad Zauq had shown Shauq his ghazals, on which basis he calls himself his ustad, and still wants Zauq to come and take advice from him. To me, it seems he is bordering on senility.

The matla of the ghazal he recited was indeed great; the rest was just so–so.

> *Likha hua hai yeh us mahjabeen ke parde par*
> *Naheen hai aisa koi is zameen ke parde par*

> So it is written so on my beloved's veil:
> 'There's none like this from mount to vale.'

To tease Ustad Zauq, Ghalib, Momin, Azurda, Sahbai and all the other ustads offered a great many 'Wah, wahs' to Mian Shauq. He thought, 'How they're applauding my verse!' little knowing they were pulling his leg. At the slightest praise, he would turn to Ustad Zauq and say, 'See? This is how a couplet is composed.' Poor Zauq would just laugh and fall silent. Some of his disciples wanted to retort, but he stopped them.

Khuda-khuda karke† when we were freed of him, the lamp came to *Azad*. His name is Alexander Headley and

---

* The imam leads prayers in a mosque.
† 'With God on our lips'—implying after a long struggle over much time.

he is French.* He was born and bred in Delhi, where he became a captain of artillery, then went to Alwar. He is about twenty-one years old, knows some daactari† and is very fond of poetry and poetic symposiums. He is a disciple of Arif's. He has only to hear of a mushaira to present himself in Delhi.

Though dressed in military uniform, he converses in Urdu. And such pure Urdu as if a Delhiite were speaking. The verses are not too bad, either. For a Frenchman to recite such poetry in Urdu is indeed a marvel.

Let his ghazal be seen:

> *Woh garm rave rahe ma-aasi hoon jahan mein*
> *Garmi se raha naam na daaman mein tari ka*
> *Kuch paon mein taaqat ho to kar dasht nawardi*
> *Haathon se maza dekh zara jeb dari ka*
> *Chehlum mein ayadat ke liye woh meri aaye*
> *Azad thekana bhi hai is bekhabari ka*

In such heated pursuit of the word's sins am I,
searing heat dried the damp off my daaman.‡
If your feet have the strength, go wander the wild,

---

* Alexander Headley has also been identified as an Englishman.

† 'Daactar', a corruption of 'doctor', and 'daactari' therefore the science of healing.

‡ As explained in the note on tropes in the ghazal, 'daaman' is the hem of a kurta or other kind of shirt, and a recurring trope in the ghazal. Here, the metaphor is that the heat (that is, the purity) of the poet's worldly pursuits has dried away any resulting sin (that is, dampness) that appeared on his daaman.

of ripping your pockets experience the passion.*
It's on *chehlum*† that he comes to see me,
is there, Azad, sense in such oblivion?

After Azad, the lamp came to Mir Shujaat Ali *Tasalli* on the opposite side. This poor fellow has rather unassuming looks, is plainly dressed and aged about sixty-four or sixty-five. He was one of Shah Naseer's favourite disciples, and considered a Jurat‡ of his age. For a long time now, he has been slipping to the edges of the world, and has moved to Qadam Shareef§. The lure of the mushaira pulls him to Delhi once in a while. His way of reciting is quite peculiar: he recites as if conversing. Take a look at his ghazal, it is as if lover and beloved are engaged in a dialogue:

Kaisi thokar jadi hai hazrat-e dil
Paon per us ke sar dharo to sahi
Jab kaha maine tum pa marta hoon
Tum gale se mere lago to sahi
Bole woh kya maze ki batein hain
Khair hai kuch pare hato to sahi

---

* 'Jeb dari' is to rip one's pockets, literally; and metaphorically an expression for passion or frenzy.
† Chehlum is the ceremony that marks the fortieth day of a person's demise. The poet is being ironic, saying that the beloved only thought of visiting his sickbed after the poet was long dead, on the day of his chehlum.
‡ Qalandar Bakhsh Jurat, an acclaimed poet of the eighteenth century. He was among the poets patronized by Sulaiman Shikoh, the exiled Mughal prince mentioned above.
§ This would have been a holy site.

Ghair ki lag ke kal woh chati se
Mujh se kahne lage suno to sahi
Is liye us ke hum gale se lage
Ke zara ji mein tum jalo to sahi

What blows have you borne, O dear heart?
Try keeping your head at his feet, at least.
When I said, 'I do die for you,
will you not even embrace me?'
He said, 'Your talk is such delight,
but such as it is, step aside please.'
Having one day embraced my *ghair*,
he said, 'Please just listen to me:
I held him only so that you
might feel a pang of jealousy!'

This ghazal was not praised as it should have been, because now it was that hour when heads were spinning from drowsiness and any discernment between good and bad had been extinguished.

The two ghazals that followed after this, well . . . they merely followed. Nobody listened with any interest nor did anyone enjoy them.

Shor recited his ghazal after Mian Tasalli. He is from Koel; Christian by community, George Peace by name. I don't know whose disciple he is, but he is, indeed, a frequent visitor to Delhi. Whatever he composes is as much as it can be.

Ajiz tha apni jaan se aiyese tera mariz
Dekhe se jis ke halaat-e Isaa tabah thi
Bul be ye bekhoodi ke khoodee se bhula diya
Warna yeh ziest marg ki apni gavah thi
Daer-o haram mein tu na de tarjeeh zaheda
Jis simt sar jhuka wohi bus sijda gaah thi

So crushed by this life was your victim,
by the sight of him Jesus was broken.
So futile in forgetful futility—
this life its own end does betoken.
Choose not between temple and mosque, O *zahid*—
where the head bows there prayer is spoken.

After him came Mohammad Askari *Nalan's* turn. Who could even hear this ninety-year-old codger's voice in the thrall of sleep! He is *Mashafi's* very first disciple and may now be considered a sacred relic. His couplets, too, are in a style as old as Adam.

Sehar ke hone ka dil ko khayaal rahta hai
Shab-e vesal bhi dil ko malaal rahta hai
Woh budguman hoon ke us but ke sae per bhi mujhe
Raqeeb ka hi sada ehtemaal rahta hai

The thought of dawn's coming troubles my heart;
even on the night of *vesal* it despairs, my heart.
I have such doubts that even my love's shadow
resembles *raqeeb's* coming, to my heart.

No sooner had Mian Nalan finished reading than the lamp arrived before Mir Saheb, and no sooner had the lamp been thus placed than every man sat up alert. Some rubbed the sleep from their eyes with their hands, others with their kurtas; some got up, sprinkled water on their faces and returned to their seats.

What of sleep and where any question of nodding off now? Mir Saheb's name animated everyone. Mirza Fakhru had long been sitting in one pose; now he changed his posture. Smiles flickered on the faces of the masters; the youngsters whispered amongst themselves.

Mir Saheb, too, inched a little ahead of his row. Mirza Fakhru said, 'Mir Saheb, that's right. Please come to the centre and recite.' With these words, he signalled to the chobdar, who picked up both the lamps and placed them in the centre of the courtyard.

Mir Saheb came up and sat directly in front of the shamiana. Who in Delhi doesn't know Mir Saheb? Where is the mushaira that isn't lit up by him, where the mehfil that isn't filled with cheer when he walks in?

There are few who would know his real name. As long as I've heard of him, I've only known him as Mir Saheb. Aged about seventy, he has a dry, shrivelled appearance, with beautiful, large eyes and thick eyelids, a parrot's beak for a nose, broad mouth, long beard and a smallish head with close-cropped hair; tall and fair complexioned.

If you were to ask, any small child in Delhi would give you a full account of his appearance. Spotless clothing always: white one-bar pyjamas, white kurta under a white

angarkha and a brocade-embroidered arkhcheen topi on
his head.

He wore an expression of great sobriety but when he
lost his temper, he would not be controlled by anyone.
Nobody, young or old, spoke to him without joking and
he, too, would offer such repartees as would make one's
head spin. He had little interest in whether his reply was to
the point or not.

In a mushaira, everyone from Badshah Salamat to
Mian Taskeen would tease him, and he would neither take
offence, nor hesitate in answering back, neither to one nor
the other. He always recited his ghazals impromptu, having
never bothered to bring one written down. There was
never any worry about a ghazal's metre; the only concern
was that his lines should rhyme. Whatever he had to say, he
would begin to say it in prose quite naturally, responding to
any objections that were raised as he went along. When he
grew tired of talking, he would round off the couplet with
radeef and *qafia*—the end rhymes.

He had only to begin reciting for objections to pour
in from all sides. But he's hardly one to be cowed, he can
fight on multiple fronts and, when unable to subdue an
opponent with his tongue alone, stands up in excitement.
No sooner had he stood up than someone would make him
sit, admonish the fault-finder and cajole Mir Saheb to take
heart. And so, once again, the process of objections would
begin!

Forget the others, Maulvi Mamluk-ul Ala Saheb enjoyed
these entanglements with him greatly; and Mir Saheb, too,

would dress Maulvi Saheb down with such vigour that should any of his students hear, Maulvi Saheb would lose all hold upon his madarsa.

Upon taking his seat before the lamps, Mir Saheb[*] surveyed the gathering and said, 'Hazraat—gentlemen— today I shall recite a *qasida* in honour of Mian Hudhud. Our Mian Mitthu has praised himself long enough, now let him listen to his *hajv*[†] with an open heart too.'

Everyone was already annoyed with Hudhud, so when they heard that he was going to be subjected to a hajv, and that too from Mir Saheb, they all said, 'Yes Mir Saheb, indeed, please recite!'

Mian Hudhud was Hakeem Agha Jaan *Aish*'s toady, firing his jibes from Hakeem Saheb's shoulders. Now, when Hakeem Saheb heard that Mir Saheb would take on Hudhud with a hajv, he became anxious, 'What if I am brought into it too? If it were a hajv by someone else, one might even respond, but who can face Mir Saheb's endless lines!' Unable to think of any other escape, he hid Hudhud behind a bolster.

When Mir Saheb looked around, he found that Hudhud had vanished. Everyone grew worried, looking this way and that. When he was nowhere to be found, he said, 'I shall defer the hajv. I will now recite my ghazal.'

---

[*] Baig notes that Mir Saheb died after the disturbances of 1857. Baig's account of him is based on eyewitnesses who had, indeed, seen Mir Saheb's legendary performances.

[†] A genre of Persian and Urdu poetry in which the subject is lampooned; what would be called a 'roast' in the American tradition of today.

Everyone said, 'Mir Saheb, Mir Saheb, why have you forsaken your intention? Read it out, Mir Saheb, for the love of God, read it! After Sauda,* the hajv has practically disappeared from Urdu. If even you pay no attention to it, there will be disaster! Our language will be left lacking.'

Mir Saheb said, 'No, bhai, no. Had Mian Hudhud been here, I would have said what I had to, to his face. To speak behind his back is not hajv but violation; and I condemn those who do such things.'

When he realized that this was Mir Saheb's disposition, Hakeem Agha Jaan was able to breathe easy once again. He, too, threw in a few words on the distinction between a hajv and mere imprecations, and thanked God for his escape.

Now Mir Saheb began his ghazal. God knows what he read; all that we understood was that *teer*, *peer* and *kheer* comprised the qafia, and *hai* the radeef. Other than this, Mir Saheb himself wouldn't be able to tell you what he read and what he meant. Whenever the qafia and radeef were uttered, it was understood that a couplet had been completed, the plaudits began, while someone held out an objection or two.

No sooner was he criticized than Mir Saheb grew agitated, and his agitation entertained everyone. Here, taste the objections and Mir Saheb's retorts:

Once Mir Saheb began expanding a misra in his ghazal, he stretched it so that it became as long and tangled as the

---

* Mirza Muhammad Rafi 'Sauda' (1713–1781) was considered a master of the hajv, with which he frequently demolished his rivals.

Devil's intestines. Maulvi Mamluk-ul Ala Saheb said, 'Mir Saheb, this misra seems to have fallen into a bahr-e taveel, a very long metre.'*

Mir Saheb said, 'Maulvi Saheb, have you ever even read a bahr-e taveel, or are you just pinning your objections on hearsay? First read *Mutawwal*, then you'll know what a long metre really is.'†

Maulvi Saheb was greatly perplexed. He said, 'Mir Saheb, what does *Mutawwal* have to do with metres? Like aiming for the knee and hitting the eye, you blurt out whatever comes to your mind!'

Mir Saheb now looked around for a champion. He looked at Maulvi Sahbai, who said, 'Maulvi Saheb, if *Mutawwal* doesn't feature long metres, what kind of metres does it have? You know you only want to silence Mir Saheb with your scholarship, that's all!'

This much aid was enough to make Mir Saheb bold as a lion. 'Indeed Maulvi Saheb, you think nobody's read *Mutawwal* except you! Arre, my dear sir, I race through it twice a day! Only yesterday I sat down to write a ghazal in its metre. I grew tired from writing: one misra I finished

---

* 'Bahr' is 'metre', and 'bahr-e taveel' is a particularly long metre, in which each line of a poem might stretch to a whole page. The effect of it might be something akin to prose or poetry written in the stream of consciousness style.

† *Al-Mutawwal*, an exegesis on rhetoric by the Persian scholar Al-Taftazani (1322–90), who wrote on a wide range of subjects, from grammar to law, and remains widely read today. The extraneousness of Mir Saheb's response might be matched by one referring to Aristotle's *Rhetoric* to settle an argument on the iambic pentametre.

in some one hundred and seventy-five pages! It's only
because my notebook ran out of paper that the misra ended;
otherwise, God alone knows where it would have gone!'

Mirza Nausha said, 'It's very true what you say, Mir
Saheb. Where has our Maulvi Saheb seen a long metre?
Ask me: do you know my nephew Khwaja Amaan? He
has written a book, *Bostan-e Khayal*, in twelve massively fat
volumes.* The whole thing was done in just twelve misras
of the long metre! *Your* misra is not in bahr-e taveel, but in
the bahr of rubai.'†

'Hain?' cried Mir Saheb, with irritation, 'Wah, Mirza
Saheb! You, too, wandered off the straight and narrow! Do
you even know the metres of the rubai? Well, tell me, what
book are they in?'

This was a rather tricky question. Mirza Ghalib hesitated
and Mir Saheb said, 'I knew it, you were raising objections
just for the sake of it! Mirza Saheb, read *Arba'in*‡—then
you'll learn what the metres of rubai are.'

An hour or so passed in such banter. Tears of laughter
cleared the sleep from people's eyes; it was as if the mushaira

---

* *Bostan-e Khayal* is a twelfth-century Persian epic; it was translated by
Khwaja Amaan 'in eight enormous tomes' according to the *Encyclopedia
of Indian Literature* (edited by Amaresh Datta, published by the Sahitya
Akademi).

† The bahr, or metre, of rubai would be quite the opposite of the more free-
flowing taveel; the rubai is a quatrain with 'an extremely rigid metrical
scheme' and several variations (Frances W. Pritchett).

‡ *Al-Arba'in Fi Usul ad-Din* or 'Al-Ghazali's Forty Principles of the Religion'
is a famous theological text by Al-Ghazali (c. 1058–1111), a Persian
philosopher. Once again, Mir Saheb's reference is quite inapt, like calling
on the authority of Francis of Assisi to settle a question of poetic form.

had gained a second wind and everyone had only just arrived. When people grew tired of raising objections and Mir Saheb of answering them, he said, out of the blue, 'Gentlemen, the ghazal is done.'

Everyone said, 'But Mir Saheb, the maqta hasn't come yet! What kind of maqta-less ghazal is this?'

Mir Saheb declared, 'A maqta is only needed by a poet who wants to announce that a ghazal is his. I have no need of any such thing. My ghazals are distinguished by this very fact: they only begin and it's clear they are Mir Saheb's and cannot be anyone else's.' As he spoke, he gathered his things and returned to his seat.

One of the lamps was now put before a poet right opposite Mir Saheb, Mirza Jaiyat Shah *Mahir*. He is the grandson of Shah Alam Badshah Ghazi Anarullah Burhana,[*] and a disciple of *Saabir*. His language is clear and his voice very sweet. He had written:

> *Hum bhi zaroor Kabe ko chalte per ab toh Sheikh*
> *Qismat se but-kade mein hi deedaar ho gaya*
> *Naseh ki baat sun-ne ka kis ko yehan dimaagh*
> *Tera hi zikr tha ke main nachaar ho gaya.*
> *Aye ham-nasheen woh hazrate Mahir na hon kaheen*
> *Ek parsa suna hai ke maikhaar ho gaya*

---

[*] Shah Alam II (1728–1806) was also Bahadur Shah Zafar's grandfather. Despite his impressive titles, he is one of the most tragic figures in the Mughal imperial family, in whose reign the Mughal empire was effectively demolished.

I too would have gone to the Kaaba, O Sheikh,
but luck brought me revelation in the *but-kada*.
Who has the time to listen to the righteous?
Just a mention of you made me the weaker.
My friend, may it not be *Mahir* himself:
a God-fearer, I hear, has become a drinker.

Mir Saheb's versification had cleared the sleep from everyone's eyes, so this ghazal was appreciated as it deserved to be, and Mian Mahir received his full share of praise for his efforts.

Next, the lamp came to Qazi Najmuddin *Barq*. He is from Sikandrabad. Aged twenty or twenty-two, he has long hair, a darkish complexion with the shadow of a beard on his cheeks. Tall and good-looking, he was dressed in white ghararedar pyjamas, a white angarkha and a dopalli topi. He is a lively, witty, sweet-spoken man of rakish, uninhibited temperament. Initially, he was a disciple of Momin Khan's. Then, at Momin Khan's instance, he began showing his verses to Mian Taskeen. His voice and delivery are melodious, and the ghazal he read was so good that all called out, 'Wah, wah!'

Bazme aghyar hai dar hai na khafa tu ho jaaye
Warna ek aah bhi khichoon to abhi hoo ho jaaye
Haram-o dair ke jhagre tere chupne se hain
Warna tu parda utha de toh tu hi tu ho jaaye
Kuch mazaa hai yeh tere rooth ke man jaane ka
Chahta hoon yun hi har roz khafaa tu ho jaaye

Tu to jis khaak ko chahe woh bane banda-e pak
Main khuda kis ko banaun jo khafaa tu ho jaaye
Aap inkar karen wasl se main dar guzra
Kuch to ho jis se tabiyat meri yaksoo ho jaaye.
Ho na ho bas mein koi kuch naheen is ki parwah
Dil-e betab pe aye Barq jo qabu ho jaye

It's an assembly of strangers, I fear you'll be offended—
or with a sigh, in a *hoo*, I would have the world ended.*
Temple and Kaaba contend since You're hidden—
lift but the curtain: it's You and You . . . unending.
What joy when you come around from your fury—
I wish, every day, you would be so offended!
Pious slaves from the mud you make, just as you please—
whom shall I make God if you are offended?
You refuse, I cheerfully end our union—
in some way at least my mind shall be rested.
I care not at all whom I may rule or not;
O Barq, let this fretful heart be commanded!

Allah–Allah, an intoxication filled the air! When he read the misra, '*Main khuda kis ko banaun jo khafaa tu ho jaaye*' the whole mehfil fell into a kind of ecstasy. Forget the others, even the masters would ask for the couplet to be read again and again, would recite it themselves and take great pleasure from it.

---

* 'Hoo' is the poet, the lover, and the worshipper's cry; a sound repeated to create a trance-like effect. Thus the Persian saying, '*Diwana ra hoo ae bas ast*', for a man in ecstasy, one 'hoo' will suffice.

Praise for him had yet to die down when the lamp was placed before Mirza Manjhle, whose pen name is *Fusoon*. He is a young man, the late Mirza Karim Baksh's son and maternal grandson of Hazrat Zill-e Subhani. What to say of him! Language is his handmaiden. He sings when he recites his ghazals—what recite? He spins magic.

I quote some couplets from his ghazal:

Allah re jazba-e dil-e muztar ke teer ka
Bahar hamare pahloo ke sufaar bhi naheen
Kuch aapi aap dil yeh mera baitha jaae hai
Zahir mein to Elahi main beemar bhi naheen

So troubled my heart, Allah re, that an arrow
leaves not a trace of the wound in my side.
It sinks as if on its own, this my heart,
Allah, of my sickness I show not a sign.

The words of the second couplet are set as beautifully as jewels on a string. And why not? After all, he is from the Fort.

After this, the lamp moving rightwards came to Lala Balmukund *Huzoor*. He is Khatri by caste and a disciple of Khwaja Mir *Dard*, some seventy or eighty years old. He has a glowing white face and white clothing; besides, a cotton towel—angocha—by his side, a white Kashmiri kerchief on his shoulders—all in all, one feels like feasting one's eyes on him. When the lamp came before him, he pleaded that he was no longer fit to recite, only to listen. When everyone insisted, he recited the following qata:

Na paon mein jumbish na hathon mein taaqat
Jo uth kheechen daaman hum us dilruba ka
Sar e rah baithe hain aur yeh sada hai
Ke Allah wali hai be-dast-o pa ka

No spring in my feet, nor strength in my arms
to rise up and tug at my *dilruba's daaman*;
crouched on the road and this is my call:
that Allah upholds those who lose their all.

He recited the qata in such a way that he became its very picture. Reciting '*Na paon mein jumbish*' he got up, but his legs wouldn't cooperate; stumbling, he sat back down. With '*Na hathon mein taaqat*' he raised his arms, but they barely rose and fell down. He read the second misra rather fast, and while reciting the third he sat like a frail and helpless man, begging for help by the road. When he raised both eyes to the skies and read the fourth misra, it was as if a spell had been cast on the gathering. Instead of praise, every tongue called out, spontaneously, '*Allah wali hai be-dast-o pa ka!*'

Ustad Zauq said, 'This is God's boon and Khwaja Mir Dard's benediction. Subhan Allah, what powerful verses! To arouse such sublime feeling in worldly people like us, you need an ustad like Mir Dard.'

After such verses, who would listen to Mirza Ghulam Mohiuddin *Ashki*'s ghazal? He is a grandson of Shah Alam Badshah Ghazi. Aged about forty. Tall and dressed in white, he is a man of pious and trustworthy appearance. Earlier, he took advice from Nizamuddin *Mamnoon* and has now become a disciple of Mufti Sadruddin's.

He had written:

Kuch wajd naheen naghma-e mutrib pe hi mauqoof
Kaafi hai yehan nala-e be rabte daraa bhi
Sajde mein gire dekh ke tasweer-e but Ashki
Maloom hua aap ka khirqaa tha reyaa ka

Bliss isn't only the strains of a song,
a bell's fitful tolling may also suffice.
Seeing the *but* fell *Ashki* prostrate,
and it was revealed: his piety was fake.

Next, the lamp came to Sahebzada Abbaas Ali Khan *Betaab*. He would be about thirty or thirty-two years old, a resident of Rampur, and a disciple of Momin Khan's. He is a great friend of Nawab Mustafa Khan *Shefta's* and had come to the mushaira along with him.

He read the ghazal at a very high pitch; it seemed like he was reading prose. The ghazal wasn't very good, but the qata was such that it cannot be praised enough. He had described the tavern so beautifully that . . .subhan Allah. Hai!

He had written:

Mamoor hai khuda ki enayat se maikada
Saqi agar naheen hai na ho mai se kaam hai
Betaab pi khuda ne tujhe bhi diye hain haath
Yeh khum hai, yeh suboo hai, yeh sheesha yeh jaam hai

The tavern thrives by the kindness of God;
our business is wine, *saqi's* absence shall pass.
Drink up, Betaab, God has given you hands:
here is cask and decanter, carafe and a glass.

Was it really necessary for Mirza Fakhruddin *Hashmat* to read at such an important mushaira? No good at composing, nor at reciting—but who could stop him! He was a prince, and Shah Alam Badshah's grandson to boot. Anyway, he read, and his clan even praised him. He was pleased.

The ghazal:

Tere bimar-e hijran ka tere bin
*Yeh aalam hai ke aalam nauhagar hai**
Mujhe rote jo dekha hans ke bole
Mere Hashmat bata kyon chashm-e tar hai

Your lovesick victim without you is such,
his existence does all existence lament.
Watching me weep, he said laughingly,
'Why, my Hashmat, are your eyes so wet?'

Now yes, the person to whom the lamp came after Betaab is young all right, but a poet; and a poet of such calibre that his name will be celebrated across Hindustan one day. What is the mushaira where Qurban Ali Baig *Salik*'s ghazal is not

---

* A pun on the word 'aalam', meaning both 'condition' and the 'world', respectively

heard with pleasure, and which of his couplets isn't asked for again and again?

Anyone who's ever attended a mushaira will recognize him from a distance. He is rather short, has very slim hands and feet, a stubby nose, tiny eyes; thick, pockmarked skin of wheatish colour, a small, straggly beard, thin on the cheeks, a little more dense on the chin, with very little hair on the head. He is about thirty. He looks just like a Turk from Bukhara. True, his clothing was different from theirs: a low-cut angarkha, narrow-bottomed pyjamas, a round white topi on his head and a long, white kerchief in his hand.

People sat up as soon as the lamp came to him. He, too, turned up the sleeves of his angarkha, straightened his topi and looked towards his ustad, Mirza Ghalib. Having received a smiling signal from that quarter, he turned to Saheb-e Alam and said, 'Do I have your permission?'

Mirza Fakhru said, 'Yes Mian Salik, recite. Where is the need for any permission?'

Salik took a piece of paper from his pocket, fiddled with it a bit and then, steadying himself, he said, 'This I do offer':

Inteha sabr azmai ki
Hai darazi shab-e judai ki
Hai burai naseeb ki ke mujhe
Tum se ummeed hai bhalai ki
Naqsh hai sang-e aastan pa tere
Dastan apni jabh-e saai ki
Hai fughan bad-e imtehan-e fughan

Phir shikayat hai narasai ki
Kya na karta visal shadi-e marg
Tum ne kyon mujh se bewafaai ki
Raaz khulte gaye mere sab per
Jis qadar us ne khud numai ki
Kitne ajiz hain hum ke paate hain
Bande bande mein boo khudai ki
Rah gayeen dil mein hasraten Salik
Aa gayee umr parsai kee

The very limits of resignation
spans *hijr*, the long night of separation.
It is the fault of my own fate,
from you I begged consideration.
Engraved upon your entrance floor
they tell my story: my prostrations.
I weep when tested to see how I weep,
and still you complain of my hesitations?
Would not *visal* have killed me with joy—
why then betray me for my annihilation?
My secrets unfolded, one after one,
as he performed his own exaltation.
How helpless am I that I go and find
in every man some sanctification?
Longings remain in my heart, O Salik,
though now it is time for pious devotion.

There was a clamour at every couplet; the majlis would go
into raptures. Every couplet would be requested over again,

every word would be praised and every literary flourish would be complimented.

Upon the third couplet, Ustad Zauq said, 'Wah Mian Salik, what can I say! Everyone has tried composing with the expression *"Jabh-e sai"* but no one has scaled the heights of your story.[*] What poetry, what flow, subhan Allah!'

Hakeem Momin Khan said, 'Mian Salik, such an old man's maqta from one so young! You have many years before you need to worry about the age of piety—don't start talking like old men already!'

Salik said, 'Ustad, I have grown old in my youth; let us see if I even witness old age or not. Besides, why abandon a subject that comes to the heart? Who will ever spend any time wondering whether he was aged or young who composed the couplet? When I am no more, its meaning will remain.'

When the flow of applause ended, the lamp came to Mirza Rahimuddin Eijaad. He is the Prince Mirza Hussain *Baksh's* son and Maulana Sahbai's disciple; about twenty-four or twenty-five years old. His compositions are good enough, though bland. He recites very well, however, and he sings very well.[†] His voice doesn't allow the weakness of his verse to reveal itself.

---

[*] 'Jabh-e sai' is to touch the forehead to the ground in prostration during prayer. In this case, the poet creates a conceit by which his forehead has touched the beloved's doorstep so often and for so long that it has left marks that tell the tale of his devotion.

[†] Baig uses the word 'gaana', or 'singing' literally, but he may have meant that the poet was skilled in the art of 'tarannum', a term that signifies a melodic recitation of poetry, halfway between reading and singing.

But khane mein tha ya ke main kaabe ke qareen tha
Aiye zahid-e nadan tujhe kya hai main kaheen tha
Har chaand ke main dost ke hamrah naheen tha
Per dil woh bala hai yeh jahan tha woh woheen tha
Tora hai yeh kuch aap ko main-ne ke jahan mein
Sabit na raha naam ka jo mere nageen tha

If in the *but-khana* or by the Kaaba I was,
O foolish *zahid*, what care you where I was?
True, in my friend's company I was not,
but this heart is such an imp, where he was, there I was.
I have broken myself in such ways in this world,
no more whole is the jewel of my name as it was.

There was little to like in the ghazal, but his singing was
a pleasure. This new fashion of reciting in song has come
from the Fort, but the masters do not approve of it.

After this, the lamp came to Nawab Alauddin Khan
Alai. He recited his ghazal at a very high pitch. A favourite
disciple of Mirza Ghalib's, he is still young. His verses are
good, and why not—whose disciple is he, after all!

Have a look at the ghazal, the ustad's style is apparent.*

Awaragane gulkada-e aaz-o aarzoo
Hasha agar tumhen sare sair o fragh hai
Rakheo sanbhal ke paon jo beena ho chashm-e dil

---

* 'Ustad ka rang ghalib hai'—possibly a pun on 'Ghalib', meaning both
the poet's ustad and, literally, 'predominant' or 'victorious'. Ghalib's style
coloured his student's verse.

Keejo sanbhal ke kaam jo roshan dimagh hai
Woh gul jo aaj hai qadah-e mauj khez-e rang.
Woh lala jo ke bagh ka chasm-o chragh hai
Gul choor kal hai sang-e jafa-e sipahar se
Goya ke ghamkad-e ka shikasta ayaagh hai
Aur lala tund e bad e hawadis se khak o khoon
Goya dil-o jigar ka kisee ke woh dagh hai
Jis ja ke tha tarana-e bulbul nishat khez
Us ja pe aaj dilshikan awaaz-e ragh hai
Maghroor-e jah se yeh kaho tum Alaiya
Kal ek sath-e khaak hai jo aaj bagh hai

O wanderers drifting in fields of desire,
woe, if you pine but to wallow in leisure.
Tread carefully, if your heart is discerning,
work carefully, if your mind knows its measure.
The rose that today fills a goblet with colour,
the poppy that rules the gardens of pleasure—
tomorrow it crushes the rose, heaven's anger,
to shreds, like a goblet of woe that is shattered;
the poppy is bloodied by winds of disaster,
like a mind or a heart dreadfully disfigured.
Once where would sing a sweet nightingale,
there do but crows now caw–caw together.
To the proud of position, tell them O Alaiya:
today's pleasure garden is tomorrow's dry desert.

The lamp had only to appear before him for Mirza
Karimuddin *Rasa* to sit up straight and read out a very long

ghazal, every bit of it insipid. [Not to be confused with our narrator, this Karimuddin is the elderly poet who was always first to arrive at and last to leave a mushaira.] Neither was the play of its words any good, nor was there any worth in its meaning. The excessive clichés were suffocating and the convoluted syntax made the heart despair.

Two couplets as examples will suffice, I think:

Baaz aa, sataa tu mujh ko bahut ishwagar naheen
Karta kisi pe zulm koi is qadar naheen
Go naza mein hoon main tere bin aye jaan-e man
Karne ki jaan bhi mere tan se safar naheen

Stop, do not torment me *ishwagar*, so
such cruelty should torment no one so.
Love of my life, I die in torment without you,
yet life will not leave my body on its own.

When he finished, it was Nawab Ziauddin Khan *Naiyar Darakhshan's* turn to read. He composes very well in Persian, but his Urdu ghazals are a bit dull.

He had written:

Pi ke girne hai khayal hamein
Saqiya lijiyo sambhal hamein
Shub jo aye na apne vaade per
Guzre kya kya na ihtemaal hamein
Dil mein muzmir hain mani-e baqi
Kisi soorat naheen zawal mujhe

Tere ghusse ne ek dum mein kiya
Murda-e noh hazaar saal mujhe
Tala-e bud se Naiyer-e Rakshan
Apne hi ghar mein hai wabal mujhe

Drink may bring a fall upon me,
Saqiya then take mercy upon me.
At night he came not as he'd vowed,
then what fears did not fall upon me!
Unsaid meanings do hide in my heart,
unsaid, they bring no harm upon me.
Your wrath in just a moment brings
nine thousand years of death upon me.
Bad fortune it is, O Naiyar-e Rakhshan,
my own home it wields a curse upon me.

After this, the lamp came to Mirza Peyare *Rafat*. He is of royal lineage, and very fond of quail fighting. He writes verses very well, and reads them very well too. Initially, he was Ehsan's disciple, now he's gone over to Maulana Sahbai. He must be around forty.

He had written:

Basan e taer-e rang-e pareeda wahshat se
Kise dimagh hai ab ashian banane ka
Na uzr tha hamein hone me khak ke gur hum
Yeh jaante ke woh daaman naheen bachane ka
Gundhi thi kaun se budmast tishna lab ki woh khak
Ke jis se khum yeh bana hai sharaab khaane ka
Ba zauq naz ko de rukhsat-e jafa ke yehan

Hamein bhi azm hai taqat ke azmane ka
Hain ek woh bhi ke tum se hai jin ko raz-o neyaz
Aur ek hum hain ke takte hain munh zamane ka

Like bright-feathered birds, fluttering wild,
who thinks of building shelter now?
I would not have feared falling to dust,
if dust on his *daaman* he would allow.
What eager lips and drunken made the clay
of which the goblet's made in this wine-house?
Let your cruel charms rule on, unbound:
I too shall test what strength I've found.
There are some you share your secrets with,
and there am I . . . staring blankly at a crowd.

The melancholy picture that the last couplet captures cannot be praised in words. There was no one who didn't repeat its second misra, swaying in ecstasy and calling out, 'Wah, wah, subhan Allah!' again and again.

Somehow, eventually, Mian Arif's number came up. Where would he have found the time to compose a ghazal while arranging the whole mushaira! Even so, he'd written something in the middle of it all, which is what he read out. To write even so much while rushed off one's feet night and day was a wonder.

The ghazal:

Uthta qadam jo aage mera nama-bar naheen
Peeche to chor aye kaheen us ka ghar naheen
Auron ko ho to ho hamein marne se dar naheen

Khat le ke hum hi jaate hain ger nama ber naheen
Be iltefatiyon ka teri shikwa kya karen
Apne hi jab ke naala-e dil mein asar naheen

Now that my feet will step forward no more,
have I left it behind me, somehow, his door?
Others might fear it, I fear not death, no,
I'll carry the message if no bearer will go.
What complaint shall I make of your sore cruelty,
when the cries of my heart do not touch you at all?

Everyone praised the matla. Ustad Ehsan said, 'Mian Arif,
I have grown old reciting verses. Lakhs of couplets have I
heard, and lakhs recited, but this idea is entirely new. And
how artfully it's been expressed! A great pleasure.'

After Mian Arif, the lamp came to Mirza Ghulam
Naseeruddin alias Mirza Manjhle. He is a prince, a disciple
of Ehsan's, and *Qanaat* is his pen name. His ghazals are quite
good. I'd say there are few poets like him among the ranks
of princes.

The ghazal:

Shauq ko kasrate nazzara se rashk aata hai
Hashr se pahle moyassar hua deedaar mujhe
Kaabe tak jane mein thi khatire zahid warna
Daer mein bhi thi sada rukhsat-e deedaar mujhe
Jins-e duzdeeda ki manind hai uljhao mein jaan
Ke na leta hai na phere hai kharidar mujhe
Raaz-e dil lab pe na lana kabhi Mansoor ke yaan
Kar diya baat ke kahne ne gunahgar mujhe

Passion itself envies all that's on show,
well before Doom, I saw His Own Glory.
For *zahid* I went to the Kaaba, although
temples did also hold visions for me.
Like a thing stolen, my life's in turmoil,
neither purchased nor returned can I be.
Unlike Mansoor, keep your heart from your tongue:
it was telling that made such a sinner of me.

As soon as the lamp came to Hakeem Agha Jaan *Aish*, people began whispering amongst themselves. Hakeem Saheb is a physician for the royal family, adorned with jewels of learning, an incarnation of accomplishment. Courteous, pleasant, soft-spoken with a cheerful countenance, he's always seen smiling. He has a jovial humour, so witty and full of good cheer that subhan Allah!

Of average height with a fine figure, a finger's length of white hair on his head and a similar beard—this looks delightful on his fair and ruddy complexion. He wore a muslin kurta, like a spread of jasmine flowers in blossom.

For some time, however, even his friends have been estranged from him. He has ruined relations with everyone by adopting Mian Hudhud as his protégé. Initially, no one paid much attention to Hudhud's nonsense, but when he began attacking the ustads, people took an aversion to Hakeem Saheb along with Hudhud. The last straw was when, at a mushaira in Ajmeri Gate, Hakeem Saheb himself attacked Mirza Nausha. He wrote this qata:

Agar apna kaha tum aap hee samjhe to kya samjhe
Maza kahne ka jab hai ek kahe aur doosra samjhe
Kalam-e Mir samjhe aur zubaan-e Meerza samjhe
Magar in ka kaha yeh aap samjhen ya khuda samjhe

If you alone know what you say—what's the good?
The pleasure of verse is to speak—and be understood.
Mir's verses and Mirza's words, these I have known:[*]
but what he says who knows—himself or God alone!

Maulvi Mamluk-ul Ala said, 'Hakeem Saheb, there are only two reasons for not understanding a couplet. Either the verse is meaningless or the listener's intelligence is weak. We all understand his verses, so why have you painted us poor souls with your brush?'

Momin Khan said, 'Bhai, I think the third line of this qata takes great poetic licence.'

Anyway, it was with great difficulty that the matter was covered up. This was the first time since that altercation that Hakeem Saheb had come to a mushaira. People had already heard Mir Saheb's declaration of war upon Hudhud. Now, when people began whispering to each other, Hakeem Saheb grew even more worried and hesitated to recite. Finally, on the insistence of Mirza Fakhru, he read this ghazal:

Sulh unse hamein kiye hi bani
Dil pe jhagra tha dil diye hi bani

---

[*] Mir Taqi 'Mir' and Mirza Muhammad Rafi 'Sauda', both renowned poets of the eighteenth century.

Zohd-o taqwa dhare rahe sare
Haath se us ke mai piye hi bani
Saath laye woh ghair ko nachaar
Paas apne batha liye hi bani
Kis ka tha pas-e shauq-e zulm aye Aiysh
En jafaon pe bhi jiye hi bani

In the end, I had to make peace with him,
we'd fought over hearts, I had to give mine to him.
Pious devotion being cast well aside,
wine from his hand I had to drink from him.
His having brought my *ghair* along with him,
calling my *ghair* to me, I had to sit with him.
Whoever longs for such torments, O *Aiysh*!
Despite the pain of it, I had to go on living.

When a ghazal is such, who will not praise it? An uproar of
'Sall-e Ala!'* and cries of 'Subhan Allah!' cleared the reader's
and listeners' hearts of all resentment. Hakeem Saheb became
the same old Hakeem Saheb he was before. No one held
a grudge against him, nor he any bitterness against anyone.
Of course, if Mian Hudhud had let himself go earlier, God
knows how the mushaira would have turned out! God bless
our Mir Saheb that he shut that bird's mouth. Well, the evil
spirit arrived but left without harming anyone.†

After Hakeem Saheb came Mirza Raheemuddin *Haya*'s
number. This is the very Mian Haya whose father, the

---

* 'Blessed be the Prophet'.
† A Persian proverb that means that a crisis ready to befall was averted.

venerable Mirza Karimuddin *Rasa*, had walked into the mushaira extolling the virtues of his progeny.* *Haya* is a pleasant tempered, sharp yet gentle and humorous man. Aged about thirty-five or thirty-six, he stays in Banaras for the most part and comes to Delhi occasionally. He looks just like the princes, except that he is clean-shaven and dressed in the Lucknowi style.

He was his father's disciple to begin with, then took lessons from Shah Naseer, and now takes his verses to Ustad Zauq. He is an excellent chess player. He learned it from Hakeem Ashraf Ali Khan; now often ambushes Momin Khan. He plays the sitaar so well, subhan Allah!—and is a good poet too, though he doesn't work hard at it. He sacrifices meaning to the sweet syrup of language.

He had brought this ghazal:

> *Maut hi chaara saz-e furqat hai*
> *Ranj marne ka mujh ko raahat hai*
> *Ho chuka wasl waqt-e rukhsat hai*
> *Aye ajal jald ah ke fursat hai*
> *Roz ki daad kaun deve ga*
> *Zulm karna tumhari aadat hai*
> *Karvaan umr ka hai rakht badosh*
> *Har nafas bang e kos-e rahlat hai*
> *Saans ek phans si khatakti hai*
> *Dam nikalta naheen musibat hai*

---

* This is meant sarcastically, of course: the father had been nothing if not critical of his son.

Tum bhi apne Haya ko dekh aao
Aaj us ki kuch aur halat hai

Death alone cures the pain of parting,
the pain of death is, to me, consoling.
Now we have met, now it's time to be going;
come quickly, my End, I am free and awaiting.
Who has the will to applaud every day?
It's a habit of yours after all, such oppressing.
The caravan of age is well on its way,
each breath is a milestone along its passing.
Each breath like a splinter with cutting edges—
what a bore that this life cannot be forsaken!
Come, you too, come and meet your *Haya*,
today his condition is deteriorating.

On the fifth couplet, his father ticked him off, saying,
'Mian Haya, you had already changed your appearance in
Lucknow, now you've changed your language too? Do you
consider *saans* (breath) feminine?'

Haya replied, 'Not at all, sir; I have followed Ustad
Zauq. He says:

Seene mein saans hogi ari do ghari ke baad

The breath will stick in my chest, in a while*

---

* Here, as in Haya's ghazal, 'saans' is used as a feminine noun—impossible to
translate into English, in which nouns are not gendered.

But would Saheb-e Alam be silenced? He said, 'Can your ustad's poetry be used against me? Let him write what he wills. Tell me, is *saans* masculine or feminine in the Fort?'

Poor *Haya* smiled and kept quiet.

Now, the lamp came to Maulana Sahbai. His scholarship is being celebrated across Hindustan. Men of this calibre are rarely born. He has thousands of disciples who often compose in rekhta. He tutors them, and wonderfully well, too, but his own verse and its excellence is in Persian. I have not read nor heard a rekhta ghazal by him; in the mushaira, too, he recited a Persian ghazal. There was great praise, but truthfully speaking, no one really enjoyed it. I can't describe how much the maqta was applauded, but those poor souls who didn't understand Persian sat looking blank. To put it frankly: this imposing of a Persian ghazal upon an Urdu mushaira was not something even I approved of.*

Aha, now if you really want to relish language, listen to Sayyid Zaheeruddin Khan *Zaheer*. He's only about thirty or thirty-five years old, but God has gifted him such a talent for poetry that—wah, wah! Ustad Zauq's advice has added a further sheen to his art.

His appearance does not reveal his character. A good height, slim figure and broad chest; darkish colour with an ample mouth, a high and finely chiselled nose, bright eyes neither too wide nor small, a round beard neither too dense nor sparse and thick wavy locks on his head. Dressed in

---

* Like the many blank faces at the mushaira, we too must admit our inability to translate this ghazal as it deserves, so have omitted it here.

an angarkha, narrow-bottomed pyjamas and a round white cap, he is good-natured and full of humour, so it is as if flowers fall off his tongue. He has a special style of reading too, a bit like the Lucknowi style of *tahtul lafz,* reciting like prose, and alongside he expands on every word with gestures.

His ghazal:

Jabeen aur shauq us ke aastan kaa
Eraada aur eraada bhi kahan kaa!
Luta hai qafla taab-o tawan kaa
Khuda hafiz hai dil ke kaarwaan kaa
Meri waamandgi manzil rasan hai
Suraghe naqsh-e pa hoon kaarwaan kaa
Rahe paband dil ke dil mein armaan
Qadam manzil ne pakra kaarwaan kaa
Utha sakte naheen sar aastan se
Ghazab hai baar-e minnat pasban kaa
Hamesha morid e barq-o bala hoon
Mite jhagra elahi ashiyan kaa
Dil-e betab ne woh bhi mitaaya
Kisi ko kuch jo dhoka tha fughaan kaa
Zaheer aao chalo ab mai-kade ko
Nikala zohd-o taqwaa hai kahaan kaa

My forehead's passion for his threshold—
there was never a more determined man!
The procession is robbed of its fortitude,
May God watch over my heart's caravan.

My weariness is what shows me the way,
my tracks show the way of the caravan.
My heart's desires stay trapped in my heart,
now that my feet follow the caravan.
I can't lift my forehead from his threshold;
how benign was the anger of the doorman!
Ever am I struck by lightning storms,
Lord let the squabble for shelter end!
My restless heart undid even that little
hope that my weeping might earn me a glance.
Zaheer, come along, let us go to the tavern,
what use are they now: abstinence, devotion?

Forget the others, even the ustads applauded his ghazal so
much that Mian Zaheer's heart unfurled with joy. The flow
of praise for the third couplet seemed like it would never
end. The poor fellow's hands must have ached from salaams.

When some peace returned, the lamp moving rightwards
came to Nawab Mustafa Khan Shefta. What can I say of him!
Considered amongst the masters of the craft, he is a disciple
of Momin Khan's but is an ustad himself. Should he praise a
couplet, its worth rises; should he listen and remain silent, the
couplet falls in others' eyes. To give full rein to both language
and meaning is the work of such men. He recites like this,
too, as if explaining every word. His enunciation is so clear
that everyone can hear him clearly, whether near or far.

Before reciting his ghazal, he looked around, adjusted
his angarkha and his topi, pulled up the sleeves of his
angarkha and recited this ghazal:

Aaram so hai kaun jahaan-e kharaab mein

Gul seena chaak aur saba izteraab mein

Sab is mein mahv aur ye sabse elaheda

Ayeene mein hai aab na ayeena ab mein

Mani ki fikr chahye soorat se kya husool

Kya faida hai mauj agar hai sorab mein

Zaat-o sifaat mein bhi yehi rabt chaahiye

Joon aftab-o roshni-e aftab mein

Woh qatra hoon ke mauja-e darya mein gum hua

Woh saaya hun ke mahv hua aftab mein

Be-bak sheva shokh tabiyat zubaan daraz

Mulzim hua hai per naheen ajiz jawaab mein

Taklif Shefta hui tum ko magar huzoor

Is waqt ittefaq se woh hain ataab mein

Who has peace in this wretched world,
the rose's heart is torn, the breeze troubled.*
All are immersed in Him, He apart from all—
the sheen is not the mirror, it is mirrored!
It matters what's within; what matters how it seems?
What use the wave that in a mirage glimmered?
Nobility and nature should be in harmony
as the sun with how the sun dazzles.
I am that drop lapped up by the sea,
the shadow that into the sun was merged.
Daring, disdainful and quick of tongue,

---

* That is, a rosebud must tear itself in order to blossom, a breeze must race about in order to fufil its function—thus nothing in this world is at peace.

he's often accused, never lost for words.
You have been troubled but *Shefta*, dear sir—
at this hour, it happens that he is angered.

The ghazal was such that who could possibly have summoned the words to praise it suitably? And yet, the praise was measured. I have always noticed that, at such important mushairas, beginners and youngsters are given heart with much praise, but when it comes time for the masters to recite, the same animation doesn't remain. Instead, a sort of sobriety creeps in. Only those of their couplets that truly deserve it are praised; if any couplet is praised without reason, the ustads are troubled. They want appreciation for only those verses they consider worthwhile themselves. If they look at any one after reading, it is only at their equals, who alone offer commendation. Others at the mushaira don't only enjoy their poetry but also learn from it. For them, these ghazals are no less than a lesson from an ustad.

After this came the turn of the prince Mirza Qadir Baksh *Sabir*. He must be some forty years old. His poetry is renowned in the Fort; he, too, is quite proud of his compositions. He is writing an account of the poets of Delhi, but it is rumoured that the whole thing has been penned by Maulana Sahbai, from beginning to end. God alone knows if this is true or false.

He has written of himself in a qata, which I quote:

Pahle ustad the Ehsan-o Naseer-o Momin
Hui Ehsan pe islah-e tabiyat meri

Phir hua hazrate Sahbai ki islah ka faiz
Taba bareek hui un ki badolat meri
Aur hum bazm rahe Momin-o Zauq-o Ghalib
Ustadon se hi hardam rahi sohbat meri
Hind ka fazl-o hunar zaat pa hai jin ki tamaam
Mante hain wohi ashkhash fazilat meri
Munaqad hoti hai jab shahar mein bazm-e inshad
Karte hain ahle sokhan waqqat-o izzat meri

My ustads were once Ehsan and Naseer and Momin;
to Ehsan my temperament took me.
Hazrat Sahbai was thereafter my blessing,
his teachings did truly refine me.
My companions were Momin and Zauq and Ghalib,
I was always in such exalted company.
Those with the virtues and learning of Hind,
they know the worth of my own poetry.
When poets do gather together in town,
those who recite do appreciate me.

Now, on the basis of this kind of verse, you may call him an ustad or call him what you will. His ghazals have the same colourless quality, and his meaning is not of any great worth either, but the whole city considers him a master. Who knows, perhaps he is; perhaps the fault lies in my own understanding.

The ghazal he read:

Nazzaraa barqe husn kaa dushwaar ho gaya
Jalwa hejab-e deeda-e bedaar ho gaya

Mahfil mein main to us lab-e gulgoon ke saamne
Naam e sharaab le ke gunahgaar ho gaya
Hael hui naqaab to tahri nigaah-e shauq
Pardaa hi jalwa gaah e rukh-e yaar ho gaya
Maloom yeh hua hai ke pursish gunah ki
Aasi gunaeh na karda gunaehgaar ho gaya
Uski gali mein aan ke kya kya uthaye ranj
Khaake shafa milee to main beemaar ho gaya
Peeri mein hum ko qata-e taalquq hua naseeb
Qamat khameeda hote hi talwar ho gaya

The blaze of beauty became difficult to see:
its splendour was veiled by the eye's audacity.
In the gathering, before those rose-red lips, I
became a sinner when of wine I did speak.
The veil was drawn, it stopped my ardent eye,
it became my *yaar's* face, that very screen.
It was one who undoing wrongdoing,
committing no crime was declared guilty.
What troubles had I to face in his alley:
as I found healing ash, so illness found me.
In the dusk of my life I found a way to be free,
my crooked back made a scimitar of me.

When he finished reading, the lamp came to Mufti Sadruddin *Azurda*. Scholars of such standing are rarely poets, and if they are, they are ustads. As many acclaimed scholars as Mufti Saheb mentors, he has many more poets under his tutelage. And poets of what renown!

Mufti Saheb composes very well, but recites as if he were delivering a lecture to his students. He speaks very softly, but the effect of his personality is such that there is absolute silence in the mushaira and, when there is praise, it is for particular couplets, in subdued tones. Of course, Mirza Nausha doesn't miss a chance to joke even with him, and even raises objections, sometimes, at which there is a convivial war of words.

His ghazal—what mature poetry!

Nalon se mere kab taho bala jahaan naheen
Kab asman zameen-o zameen aasmaan naheen
Afsurda dil na ho dar-e rahmat naheen hai bund
Kis din khula hua dar-e pir-e mughaan naheen
Shab us ko haal dil ne jataya kuch is tarah
Hain lab to kya, nigaeh bhi hui tarjumaan naheen
Aye dil, tamam nafa hai sauda-e ishq mein
Ek jaan ka zeyan hai so ayesa zeyaan naheen
Katti kisi tarah bhi naheen yeh shab-e firaq
Shayad ke gardish aaj tujhe asmaan naheen
Kahta hoon us se kuch main nikalta hai munh se kuch
Kahne ko yon toh hai bhi zubaan aur zubaan naheen
Azurda hont tak na hile us ke roo baroo
Mana ke aap sa koi jadoo beyaan naheen

When did my cries not overturn the world,
earth and sky and sky and earth not overturn?
Do not lose heart, the doors of mercy never close,
whenever is the *pir-e mughan's* door unopen?

Last night my heart set out its plight in such a way,
what of lips, even eyes could not have so spoken.
O heart, there's only profit in the business of love,
you lose only a life, it is of no importance.
The night of separation, it just doesn't pass,
could it be, the very axis of the world has broken?
I say one thing, the words my lips form are another;
a tongue to speak with I have, no tongue to speak in.
You could not move your lips, *Azurda*, in his presence,
though surely no one matches you for your eloquence!

For Nawab Mirza Khan *Dagh* to read after an ustad like
Azurda is unusual. The thing is, however, that everyone
likes Dagh and encourages him; they know that this very
Dagh will be Hindustan's brightest star one day. For another
thing, thanks to Mirza Fakhru's care, he was placed among
the ustads.* Besides, he recited such a ghazal that even the
ustads were impressed by it. A ghazal of such quality from a
boy of seventeen or eighteen, and for him to recite it with
such confidence was indeed a wonder.

If you ask me, there are few who have the good fortune
to be able to use language the way Dagh does. Just look at
the playfulness of his language, the vigour and flow of his
theme and imagination, and say 'Wah, wah!':

---

* Recall that Dagh had arrived at the mushaira with Mirza Fakhru, and that
Zauq had called the young poet to sit by his side. Besides, it was thanks to
his relationship with Mirza Fakhru that Dagh had such free access to the
best poets of the time.

Saaz yeh keena saaz kya jaanein
Naaz wale nayaaz kya jaanein
Shama roo aap go hue lekin
Lutf-e so gudaz kya jaanein
Kub kisi dar ki jabha sai ki
Sheikh sahab namaaz kya jaanein
Jo rahe ishq mein qadam rakhkhen
Woh nasheb-o faraz kya jaanein
Poochiye maikashon se lutf-e sharab
Yeh maza pakbaz kya jaanein
Jin ko apni khabar naheen ab tak
Woh mere dil ka raaz kya jaanein
Hazrate Khizr jab shaheed na hon
Lutf-e umr-e daraz kya jaanein
Jo guzarte hain Dagh per sadmein
Aap banda nawaz kya jaanein

What know malice-mongers of making music;
what know the pampered of beseeching!
Your face may glow as a candleflame does,
what know you of melting from yearning!
When has his forehead touched any threshold;
what does Sheikh saheb know of praying!
Those who've trodden the path of love,
what care they for ease or for suffering!
Ask drinkers for the charms of drink,
what know the chaste of wallowing!
Those who know not themselves as yet,
what know they of my heart's rending!

Unless he's martyred—Hazrat-e-Khizr*—
what can he know about ageing!
The shocks, on Dagh, that keep landing,
you sire, what would you know of them!

Allah, Allah! That pleasant hour and that young voice, those enchanting notes, those words so beautifully put together, and most of all, Dagh's innocent face—all of this gave us a strange gratification. There was no one in the gathering who was not enthralled, who would not call out, repeatedly, reflexively, jazak Allah, subhan Allah, sall-e Ala! Mirza Fakhru was so affected, he would shift in his seat, over and over again, happy in his heart without showing it. The ghazal ended without anyone even realizing it was over.

The frenzy receded when the lamp came to Hakeem Momin Khan. Everyone fell silent to listen to this master of rekhta. He picked up the lamp and moved it a little ahead, steadied himself, ran his fingers through his hair and tilted his cap, tidied the crease of his sleeves and began to recite this ghazal with an enchanting melancholy:

Ulte who shikwe karte hain aur kis ada ke saath
Betaaqti ke tane hain uzr-e jafaa ke saath
Bahre ayaadat aye woh lekin qazaa ke saath
Dam hi nikal gaya mera awaz-e pa ke saath

---

* A saint in Islamic tradition, Khirz is sometimes described as having attained immortality.

Manga kareinge ab toh dua hijr-e yaar ki
Aakhir to dushmani hai asar ko dua ke saath
Hai kis ka intezar ke khwab-e adam se bhi
Har bar chaunk padte hain awaaz-e pa ka saath
Sau zindagi nisaar karun ayesi maut per
Yun roe zaar zaar tu ahle aza ke saath
Be pardaa pas-e ghair use baitha na dekhte
Uth jaate kash hum bhi jahan se haya ke sath
Us ki gali kahan yeh to kuch bagh-e khuld hai
Kis ja yeh mujh ko chod gai maut la ke saaath
Allah re gumrahi but-o butkhaana chod kar
Momin chala hai kabe ko ek parsa ke sath

Instead, he complains, and oh how stylishly,
I am assaulted with excuses for his cruelty.
He came to ask if I was well, a deadly enquiry:
my heart did cease to beat upon the sounding of his feet.
I shall only pray for *hijr-e yaar* from this day on,
my prayers and their answers seem to share no amity.
Who is it that I await, that in this very shade of death,
I am startled by the sound of any passing feet?
For such a death I would gladly give up a hundred lives,
should you mourn along with them who at my passing
weep.
I see him seated by the *ghair*, and O unveiled is he!
Would that I had left the world before he sheds his
modesty.
This is not his lane, only a garden, paradise merely!
What kind of place has death chosen to abandon me?

Allah re, losing his way and leaving the *but-khana*,
Momin goes to Kaaba now in virtuous company.

Poetry? It was magic. Everyone was entranced. Momin
Khan was enjoying his own writing, too. His fingers would
run faster through his hair when he read a couplet he liked
better. When still more animated, he would wrap a lock
around his fingers and twirl it round and round. If someone
offered praise, he would bow his head a little and give them
a smile.

His style of reciting was unique, too. He would hardly
gesture at all with his hands. And how could he, when his
hands were never free of his hair? But yes, he could make
magic with the modulation of his voice and the intimations
of his eyes.

When the ghazal ended, all the poets praised it. He
smiled at them, and said, 'It is this kindness of yours that is
the reward for all my work. Without it, as I have said before:

Hum daad ke khwahaan hain naheen talib-e zar kuch
Tahseen-e sukhan fahm hai Momin salaa apnaa

Just praise I desire, no wealth in reward;
praise from the discerning is Momin's reward.

The lamp then came to Ustad Ehsan. I had thought he
might not even be audible, but upon the lamp's arrival he
became a different person entirely. He read the ghazal in
such stentorian tones that his voice resounded across the

majlis. At some couplets he would address Momin Khan,
at others Mirza Nausha or Ustad Zauq; and he had such an
aura that whoever he addressed was obliged to offer praise.
The radeef was tough and the qafia difficult, but his mastery
must be commended because, despite the difficulties, the
ghazal as a whole was grand.

Hai! He wrote:

Tu kyon hai girya kunaan aye mere dil-e mahzoon
Na ro na ro ke na tujh ko kabhi rolaye khuda
Buto batao toh tum kya khuda ko do-ge jawaab
Khuda ke bandon pe yeh zulm banda-hai khuda
Raza pe teri hoon din raat aye sanam masroof
Jo is pe tu na ho raazi, na ho raza-e Khuda
Buton ke kooche mein kahta tha kal yehi Ehsan
Yehan kisi ka naheen hai koi sewai khuda

O why are you so weeping, my harshly treated heart?
Do not cry, do not cry, never cry by will of God.
Tell me *buts*, how shall you explain yourselves to God?
Such tyranny on God's own men! O you people of
God . . .
Busy am I, night and day, seeking *sanam* what pleases you,
if you aren't pleased, let it be . . . it may not be the will
of God.*

---

* The idiom 'raza–e Khuda' is used to imply that something could not be
 done as it was not the will of God. Ehsan plays on 'raza' (desire or will)
 along with 'raazi' (willing, agreeable) in this couplet.

So in idol quarters was Ehsan himself speaking:
'Here no one is anyone's, excepting only God!' *

When Ustad Ehsan finished reading, it was Mirza Ghalib's turn. The atmosphere was utterly transformed. Dawn was rising. As soon as the lamp came to him, he said, 'Sahabo, let me tune the notes of my Bhairavi.'†

With these words, he recited his ghazal in such enchanting, affecting tones that the whole gathering was rapt. His voice was very high and doleful. It seemed as if he found no one in the majlis who recognized his worth, and this gave his ghazal an undertone of supplication.

The ghazal:

Dil-e nadaan tujhe hua kya hai?
Aakhir is dard ki dawa kya hai?
Hum hain mushtaq aur woh bezaar
Ya elaahi yeh maajra kya hai?
Main bhi munh mein zubaan rakhta hoon
Kaash poocho ke muddoa kya hai?

---

* Again, a beautiful play on words that suggests that the *but* (that is, the *mashooq*, the beloved) and *khuda* are one. These mashooqs will never really belong to you, even though you worship them, writes Ehsan, continuing to a larger philosophical conclusion: no *but* will ever belong to anyone, so put your faith in God alone.

† Raga Bhairavi is traditionally performed in the morning, thus Ghalib's reference to it, since he is reciting at dawn. It is also the case, as pointed out to the translators by Ranjit Hoskote, that this raga traditionally closes a concert, and this reference to it might be Ghalib's way of hinting that it is his ghazal (and not that of his rival Zauq) that marks the 'real' end of the mushaira. We are grateful to Ranjit Hoskote for this witty interpretation.

Jab ke tujh bin naheen koi maujood
Phir yeh hangaamaa aye khuda kya hai?
Yeh pari chehra log kaise hain?
Ghamza-o ishwa-o adaa kya hai?
Shikan-e zulf-e ambareen kyon hai?
Nigah-e chashm-e surma sa kya hai?
Hum ko un se wafa ki hai ummeed
Jo naheen jante wafa kya hai
Haan bhalaa kar teraa bhalaa hogaa
Aur darvesh ki sada kya hai!
Jaan tum per nisaar kartaa hoon
Main naheen jaanta duaa kya hai
Main-ne maanaa ke kuch naheen Ghalib
Muft haath aye to buraa kya hai!

My unwise heart, what has happened to thee?
Where is the balm for such agony?
I am full of longing, he is sick of me;
O my Lord, how is this meant to be?
I too hold a tongue in my mouth, I do,
if only you'd ask 'What do you seek?'
When no one exists in the world except you,
then why, O Lord, this uproar around me?
Who are these people of angelic guise,
of amorous looks, of poise, coquetry?
Why are these curls scented with ambergris?
What is this gaze lined with kohl meant to be?
I hope for faithfulness from such as these
who know not what faithfulness is meant to be.

Do good indeed and good shall be yours,
what else is the dervish's litany?
My life, that I do sacrifice unto you,
but prayer, to me, is a true mystery.
Nothing is, Ghalib, that I concede,
but if it came free, what harm can it be!

Having finished reading, he smiled and said, '*Ab is per bhi na woh samjhein to phir un se khuda samjhe*: now if he does not understand even with this, then let God take account of him!'

Hakeem Agha Jaan got the hint, and said, '*Mirza Saheb, ghaneemat hai ke tum is rang ko aakhir zara samjhe*: Mirza Saheb, it is a blessing that you have understood something of this style, finally!'

Thus, the jokes continued along with the applause, and the lamp came to Ustad Zauq. Ustad looked at Mirza Fakhru and said, 'Saheb-e Alam, should I recite a ghazal, or shall I submit the qata that came to me yesterday? God knows what happened last night, I just couldn't sleep. As I tossed and turned, it became morning. I experienced something of the flavour of shab-e hijr, and in that struggle, a qata dawned. I shall recite it if you permit.'

Mirza Fakhru said, 'Ustad, today's mushaira is free of any rules. Recite a ghazal, recite a qaseeda, recite a qata, recite what your heart desires, but recite something you must!'

Ustad Zauq sat up and recited the qata in such a deep and pleasant voice that the gathering resonated with its sound. His style of reciting heightened the effect of his poetry.

Kahoon kya Zauq ahwaal e shab-e hijr
Ke thi ek ek ghari sau-sau maheene
Na thi shab daal rakkhaa thaa ek andher
Mere bakht-e seah ki teergi ne
Tap-e gham shama san hoti na thi kum
Aur aate the paseene per paseene
Yehi kahta tha ghabra ker falak se
Ke aoh be mehr bud akhtar kameene
Kahaan main aur kahan yeh sub magar thei
Meri janib se tere dil mein keene
So is zulmat ke parde mein kiye zulm
Are zaalim teri keena wari ne
Evaz kis bada noshi ke mujhe aaj
Pade yeh zahr ke se ghont peene
Hawaas-o hosh jo mujh se qareen thei
Qareene se hue sab be-qareene
Meri seena zani ka shor sun ker
Phate jaate thei humsaeon ke seene
Uthaya gaah aur gahe bathaya
Mujhe be-tabi-o be-taqti ne
Kaha jab dil ne tu kuch kha ke so rah
Bahut almas ke tode nageene
Na toota jaan se qalib ka rishta
Bahut hi jaan todi jan kuni ne
Bahut dekha na deklaya zara bhi
Tulooye subh se munh roshni ne
Kaha ji ne mujhe yeh hijr ki raat
Yaqeen hai subh tak degi na jeene
Lage paani chuane munh mein aansoo

Padha yaseen sarhane bekasi ne
Magar din umr ke thode se baqi
Laga rakhkhe thei meri zindagi ne
Ke qismat se qareeb-e khana mere
Aazaan masjid mein di bare kisi ne
Basharat mujh ko subh-e wasl ki di
Azaan ke sath yumn-o farrukhi ne
Hui ayesi khushi Allah-u akbar
Ke khush hokar kaha yeh khud khushi ne
Muazzin marhaba berwaqt bola
Teri aawaaz Makke aur Madeene

Zauq, what can I say of *shab-e hijr*—
that every minute was months or longer?
It was no night yet darkness had fallen
from the gloom my destiny conjured.
Aflame, my sorrow's heat would not dim,
and I did sweat and sweat even further.
Startled so I would rave at the skies,
that O ye ill-starred heartless villain,
although what am I, a nothingness, yet
for me such malice your heart did harbour!
Such cruelties hid by curtains of darkness
you wrought O *zaalim* out of your rancour.
For which wine-drinking offence of mine
had I to sip this poisonous liquor?
All sanity, sense that once I had
in order, now was all disordered.
Hearing the violent beating of my heart

would tear the breast of another asunder:
it made me get up and then again sit,
such was my weakened, restless nature.
'Drink,' when my heart said, 'poison and sleep—
jewels have you long enough now gathered',
the bond between body and soul did not break
by death's agonies although I was tortured.
I looked and I looked but was never shown
the rising of dawn reveal its bright splendour.
My heart said to me, O this night of *hijr*
will not let you live till the morn, it is certain;
as tears, like water, flowed into my mouth,
at my side, Helplessness *yaseen* did tender.[*]
Still a few days of my time did remain,
my life was yet spared, a little bit longer:
by luck, as it was, not far from my house
a man called out from a mosque for prayer;
glad news of the coming of dawn came to me
with the *azaan*, of fulfilment and favour.
Such happiness blessed me, Allah-u Akbar,
that Happiness did itself say with euphoria:
'Hail the muezzin how timely he's spoken!
May your voice carry to Mecca, Medina!'[†]

He had just reached the last couplet when a voice came
from the neighbouring mosque, calling 'Allah-u Akbar,

---

[*] The yaseen is a Quranic verse traditionally recited at the time of death.
[†] Another layer of meaning for this line would be 'May your voice be as
blessed as Mecca and Medina.'

Allah-u Akbar, Allah-u Akbar, Allah-u Akbar!'—and with it every mouth formed the words, '*Teri aawaaz Makke aur Madeene*'.

When the azaan ended, everyone raised their hands to pray. Once the prayer was done, Mirza Fakhru said, 'Gentlemen, what a strange serendipity: the mushaira began with a fateha and now it ends with one.'

With these words, he blew out the two lamps, which had done their rounds and returned to him. As soon as the flames were extinguished, the heralds called out, 'Gentlemen, the mushaira has ended!'

At this, everyone stood up to leave. First, Mirza Fakhru rode away and then everyone took their leave one by one. In the end, Zain-ul-Abdeen Khan and I remained. I thanked him.

He said, 'Mian Karimuddin, it was the goodness of your intentions that ensured that such a big mushaira went off without any trouble. Your work was accomplished and my yearning fulfilled. Khuda hafiz!'

Taqdeer

Alas!

Darmaandgi mein yaa rab kuch ban pare to janoon,
Jab rishta begirah tha nakhun girah kusha tha

If there were a way out, in my helplessness, I would take it;
as my ties were untangled, my nails were caught in knots.

The next day, everything was taken away. Once again, the same old clutter-clatter of the press and the clang-clang of its machines. I announced another mushaira the following month, had notices distributed for it, too—but only a handful of people turned up. Finally, I had to end these gatherings.

The press suffered some losses. Then, some of our employees took advance payments and sat on them. And lastly, a few days later, some of my illiterate and dishonest partners defrauded me and took over the press. Although I had thought that I would surely get justice if I filed a suit, even that plan was left unfulfilled when various other calamities befell me.

The manuscript of that mushaira is left abandoned. Let us see when it is published and who publishes it.

The seating arrangement of the poets

Top side (left → right): Eijaad, Rasa, Rafat, Qamaat, Haya, Zaheer, Sabir, Dagh, Ehsan, Zauq, Ramz, Ghalib, Momin, Azurda, Shefta, Sahbai, Aish, Arif, Darakhshan, Alai, Salik

Left side (top → bottom): Hashmat, Ashki, Fusoon, Mahir, Nalan, Tasalli, Shauq, Bedil, Bismil

Right side (top → bottom): Betaab, Huzoor, Barq, Mir Saheb, Shor, Azad, Taeb, Taskeen, Tishna

Bottom side (left → right): Bismil, Jafri, Tanveer, Yekta, Josh, Tajalli, Kamil, Qalq, Tasweer, Aouj, Nazneen, Yal, Ashiq, Tamkeen, Tabish, Aouj, Taashshuq, Raqm, Aziz, Shohrat, Hazeen, Tishna

Acknowledgements

We would like to thank the people who have read various drafts of this manuscript over the years: Professor Khalid Mahmood, Dr Swapna Liddle, Priya Doraswamy and Ranjit Hoskote. Thank you for giving us so generously of your time and expertise.

Thank you also to the team at Penguin: Ambar Sahil Chatterjee, Shiny Das, Ananya Bhatia, Rea Mukherjee, and Shaoni Mukherjee, who have all, in different ways, shepherded this book to publication.

Finally, we appreciate young master Imran Ahmad Rizvi's technical contribution towards the making of the chart of the mushaira's seating arrangement.